# THE MAJOR'S FINAL MISSION

## A Civil War Novel

Jack L. Dickinson
Kyle Dickinson

ISBN 13: 978-0-9774116-8-9

**Disclaimer**
This book is a work of fiction; a novel.  None of the characters were real people.  No similarities to anyone living or dead is intended. While the events in this fictional account take place during a real period of history at the end of the Civil War, (April & May,1865,) the events never occurred. The Confederate and Union Army military units mentioned never existed. It is totally an invented story. But I hope you will agree, an intriguing one.

Printed in the United States of America

To order additional copies of this book, contact:
Martha Kay Dickinson
6221 Highland Drive
Huntington, WV 25705
Email: marthakd@earthlink.net

# The Major's Final Mission

A Civil War Novel

# April

| Sun | Mon | Tue | Wed | Thu | Fri | Sat |
|-----|-----|-----|-----|-----|-----|-----|
| 26 | 27 | 28 | 29 | 30 | 31 | 1 |
| 2 | 3 | 4 | 5 | 6 | 7 | 8 |
| 9 | 10 | 11 | 12 | 13 | 14 | 15 |
| 16 | 17 | 18 | 19 | 20 | 21 | 22 |
| 23 | 24 | 25 | 26 | 27 | 28 | 29 |
| 30 | | | | | | |

# 1865

# The Major's Final Mission
## A Civil War Novel

## Dramatis Personae
### (Cast of characters)

Major Henry Stuart Ward, 35th Virginia Infantry, CSA

Lt. Andrew "Drew" Peters, sharpshooter, also 35th Va. Infantry, CSA

Sgt. Elijah "Lige" Stephens, 29th Battalion Va. Sharpshooters, CSA

Pvt. Michael Thompson, scout, 2nd Battalion Va. Partisan Rangers, CSA

Pvt. William "Will" Wells, scout, 2nd Battalion Va. Partisan Rangers

Harrison C. Lane, governor of North Carolina

Dan Collins, bodyguard, courier, investigator for Governor Lane

Helen Ward, the major's deceased wife

Ardelia "Delia" Simmons, editor/ publisher of small-town newspaper

"Andy," Henry Ward's loyal and battle-conditioned horse.

Other characters met along the path, both good and evil.

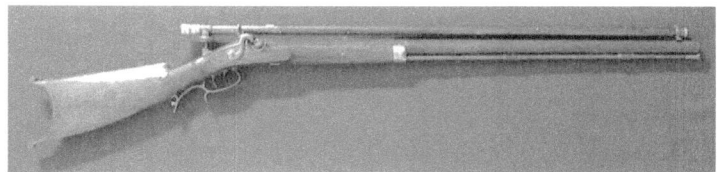

**Henry Stuart Ward,** major, 35th Virginia Infantry, CSA, (also known as 35th Regiment Virginia Volunteers,) was born in 1834, on his parents' farm in Bedford County, Virginia. He began reading at an early age, and in spite of the demands of a large farm, he attended the local school until he was thirteen. At that point, Henry went to work full-time on the farm. His father was injured about that time from a fall off a skittish horse. This accident resulted in a fractured hip, and Henry gradually assumed the majority of his father's responsibilities on the farm. At the age of twenty-one, when his three younger siblings were able to carry their load of chores, he rode overland to the Mississippi River, where he caught a steamboat heading downriver to New Orleans. After bouncing around several short-term jobs, including a few months in a newspaper office, Henry found work in a law office. He spent two years as a clerk under the tutelage of an established lawyer, who wanted him to also become a lawyer. This was quickly broken off by a letter from Ward's mother, relating that his father was gravely ill, and he was needed to return home and take charge of running the family farm. He immediately returned to his home in Virginia, and his father passed away a few months later. Henry managed the family farm until the start of the Civil War. He married Helen Snidow, daughter of another farmer in Bedford County, just before he entered the Confederate Army. When he went off to war, his sister, Rachel, and her husband Matthew Grimes, moved in with their mother to help her with the farm. **Weapons of choice**: In his first skirmish he picked up a Griswold, then later a damaged Colt, and in 1864, a .44 caliber Remington New Model Army, he picked off of a dead Yank. And always a belt knife of some kind, by 1865 this was a large Bowie knife.

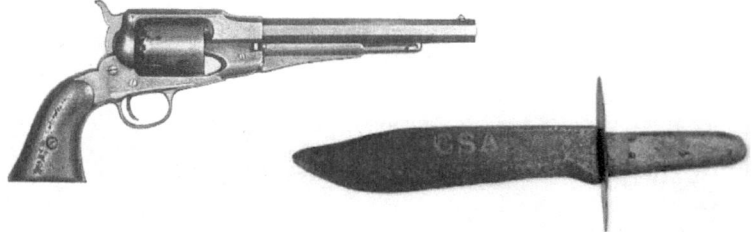

The Major's .44 cal. Remington, and his well-used Bowie knife.

4

**Andrew C. "Drew" Peters**, lieutenant, also 35th Virginia Infantry, and like Henry, John was also born and raised on a farm, albeit smaller and located in Monroe County, western Virginia. Peters came from a long line of soldiers. His great grandfather had fought in the Revolution, and his grandfather in the War of 1812. Early on, he learned to ride horses and loved to hunt. Born in 1841, and with little schooling, he taught himself to read and write. About 1859, he joined a logging crew where he chopped trees and helped assemble the logs into rafts, to float down the New River to a sawmill. Early in the war, he joined a Confederate cavalry unit and supplied his own horse, which was common in the South, and for which he was paid fifty dollars by the army. It was shot out from under him in 1862. A month later, he joined the 35th Virginia infantry, the same unit that two of his cousins from western Virginia belonged to. He rapidly became a well-respected officer and served as a messenger for Major Ward. **Weapons of choice:** In his first year, a hodge-podge of pistols. In 1864 he picked off a Union sharpshooter and took ownership of his globe-sighted, .38 caliber rifled musket, with double-set triggers. Actually the globe-sight looked like a long brass tube with lenses on either end, mounted above the rifle barrel. This was the forerunner of the modern telescopic sight. This combination was the Civil War sniper rifle. He also carried a battered, 6-shot, .36 caliber, Allen & Thurber pepperbox pistol, and a Bowie knife.

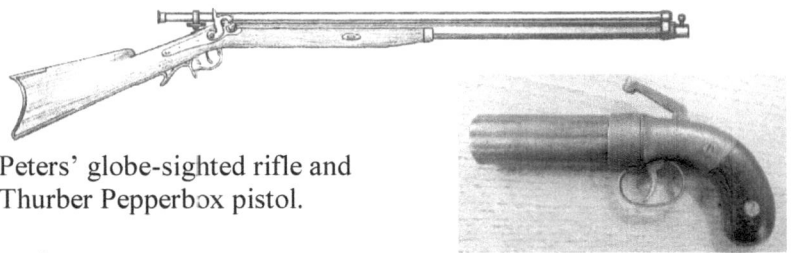

Peters' globe-sighted rifle and Thurber Pepperbox pistol.

**Elijah "Lige" Stephens**, sergeant, 29th Battalion Virginia Sharpshooters, was the least vociferous and therefore the least known of the squad. The only tidbit he had ever uttered about his past was that he was from Giles County, in western Virginia. Private Michael Thompson, who had originally been a soldier in the 29th Battalion Sharpshooters, recounted the first time he met Stephens. The unit was encamped near New Market, and Stephens simply walked into camp near dusk and stated he wanted to join, and stated he was not only a crack shot, but had excellent night vision. The next morning they challenged him to prove just how good a shot he really was. Their best sharpshooter put one bullet "from some distance" into the knot hole of a tree. When it was Stephens' turn, he fired, but everyone thought he had missed. He said "walk up to the tree, and dig out the two bullets in the one hole. Mine will be the last one in." To their amazement he was right. They instantly made him a member of their company. In 1865, his parents were still living in Giles County. **Weapons of choice:** In addition to his ordinary three-band, .58 caliber, Richmond Armory musket, his favorite was his LeMat revolver. The LeMat was a unique weapon, which was a .36 caliber black powder revolver, with a 20 gauge shotgun barrel underneath the .36 caliber barrel. It was referred to as "the Grapeshot gun." A similar pistol had been Gen. P.G.T. Beauregard's weapon of choice. Stephens also carried a knife, but it was a dagger with a long, thin, two-edged blade, that usually resided in Stephens's right boot.

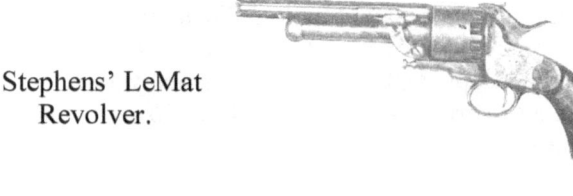

Stephens' LeMat
Revolver.

**Michael "Mike" Thompson,** private, 2nd Battalion Virginia Partisan Rangers, was actually born in Kentucky about 1840. Supposedly while living in Kentucky, he became an excellent scout and trail finder. He had the reputation of being able to find faint trails and cowpaths that others would overlook. His family moved to Wythe County, Virginia, sometime before the war, where they took over a combination sawmill and grist mill. He joined the 2nd Battalion mainly because his older brother and his cousin had joined that unit. While the partisan ranger units had an unsavory reputation, Thompson maintained that the 2nd Battalion always held a high degree of integrity, honesty, and respect in their dealings with civilians. Ward had evidently encountered Thompson before the war, which he divulged once over too many whiskeys. They had had some type of encounter on a steamboat on the Mississippi, bound for New Orleans. **Weapons of choice:** Thompson had obtained a short-barreled, .58 caliber, Tower Enfield cavalry musket, which had been smuggled in from England, through the Union blockade. It had a short, 21 inch barrel. Rumor was that he had won it in a midnight poker game. He also carried a 5-shot, .36 caliber Colt revolver. It was the "police model," which was a smaller and lighter version of the six-shot Colt Army, and easier to carry and conceal. His cutlery was a huge folding clasp knife, which resided in his boot.

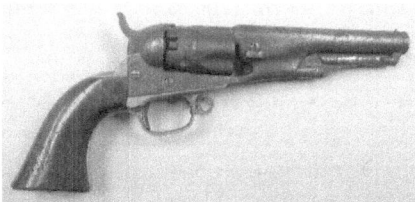

Thompson's .36 cal. Colt Police revolver.

**William "Will" Wells**, scout for the 2nd Battalion Virginia Partisan Rangers, either didn't have a true rank, or he just didn't want to talk about it. He said he had never worn a uniform of any kind. Wells was the youngest of the squad, but always evaded the question of just how young he really was. He had been born and raised just over the state line in North Carolina, and it was hoped he could be of some use as a scout on this last mission. He had originally joined the 10th North Carolina Battalion of infantry, a loose outfit that was never organized or recognized, and had wandered around for a while, and eventually met up with Michael Thompson in Virginia, where they joined the Partisan Rangers. They became friends and had been together on one of the squad's earlier secret missions. **Weapons of choice:** Wells was attached to his sawed-off shotgun, which he maintained was the right weapon for close up action. Like Thompson, he also carried a 5-shot, .36 caliber Colt Police revolver. His cutlery was a large hunting knife, which had had the last two inches of the blade broken off, making the weapon look doubly threatening. He housed it prominently in his belt.

Wells'
Double-
barreled,
sawed off
shotgun.

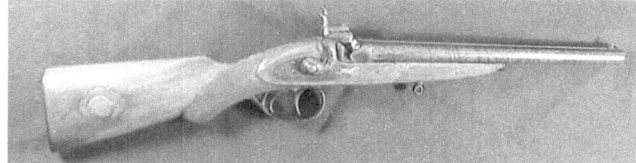

**Harrison Cincinnatus Lane**, governor of North Carolina. At age 41, he was perhaps the youngest governor in the Confederate States. His middle name was in honor of a great Roman general. Like most politicians of that time, he had practiced law in the 1850's, his law office being in Asheville. He was a strong Unionist, but sided with the Confederacy when war broke out. At that time he was serving as a representative from North Carolina, in the U. S. House of Representatives. He quickly organized a Confederate company named the "Carolina Roughs," and rose to the rank of colonel of the regiment. But one year into the war he went back into politics, being elected governor of North Carolina in 1862. He took a strong stand on several controversial war-time topics: he was opposed to Confederate States conscription to fill the ranks. He was a proponent of individual rights and local self-government, which put him at odds with President Jefferson Davis, although Davis greatly respected Lane's abilities and influence. Lane also argued that most North Carolina soldiers had been "raised for local defense," and therefore the Confederate government had violated the terms of their enlistment agreement by sending the troops out of state. He was re-elected governor in 1864. By April of 1865, his family consisted of wife Rosalee, their seventeen year old daughter Charlotte, and their ten year old son Robert. While Lane was governor at Raleigh, both Rosalee and Charlotte had worked as nurses in one of the Raleigh hospitals.

**Ardelia "Delia" Vaughan Simmons,** 28 years old in 1865, had early on achieved a good academy education at a girl's academy in Richmond. Intelligent and quick, she was not shy. Just before the start of the war, she had married Michael Simmons, a young man who inherited his father's small newspaper in Falls Bluff, Va. He joined the Confederate infantry soon after the start of the war and was killed in action at the Battle of Cloyd's Mountain on May 9, 1864. Not by choice, Ardelia became one of the "war widows" who inherited her husband's business. For the next year she struggled to keep the newspaper from going under. By her strong will and crafty business approach, it was working (barely.)

## Prologue

By April, 1865, the Confederacy was on its last legs. After a long siege, Union General U. S. Grant had captured Petersburg, Va., which was the back door to the Confederate Capitol of Richmond. As the fall of Richmond became imminent, on "Evacuation Sunday" (April 2, 1865), President Davis, his Cabinet, and the Confederate defenders abandoned Richmond and fled south. The city finally fell to Union forces the next day, with large portions of the city destroyed by fires set during the evacuation.

When Gen. Robert E. Lee surrendered on April 9, 1865, he was not in command of all the Confederate armies. He surrendered the Army of Northern Virginia, which was the most well-known army, and the one that had won the most victories. His army had lost half of its strength in the previous six months. He surrendered a little over 28,000 men. News spread of the favorable terms of surrender that he had received from Union Gen. Ulysses Grant, allowing the men to return to their homes and letting the officers, cavalrymen, and artillerymen keep their swords and horses if the men agreed to lay down their arms. Gen. Grant agreed to parole the entire Army of Northern Virginia rather than take them as prisoners. Grant even supplied food to the Rebels, who were desperately low on rations. That left Gen. Joseph E. Johnston as the top commander of the Confederate armies remaining in the field, and Gen. Kirby Smith with his smaller Army of the Trans-Mississippi.

## Chapter 1

It was that last quiet hour just before dawn.  Major Henry Ward idly poked the campfire with a long stick, sending several sparks toward the sky.  One of the horses, probably Andy, made a soft whinny.  It was that time of the morning when military men since time immemorial thought of the coming battle.  The major looked over his men, two of whom were asleep in their blankets near the fire, and the other two asleep, leaning against trees.  But would there be any more battles?  Lee had surrendered three days before.

After this last secret mission, part of the plan was the major and his squad would meet up with Gen. Joseph E. Johnston and his Army of Tennessee, further south.  But the major couldn't really see Johnston holding out more than a few weeks after Lee's surrender.  He poked the campfire again and watched the collection of red embers fly into the darkness.

And he thought of Helen, as he gritted his teeth.  Why was his vision of her always this one?  The wagon and horse were standing in the middle of the dusty road, the horse with his head lowered, as if ashamed.  His wife of two years lying in a pile of petticoats and cotton.  Her neck had been broken when the rear wagon wheel came off and she was thrown to the side of the road.  Of course the odd thing was the little smile on her lips, just the same smile she had worn when sleeping beside him.  She had been only 24 years old.  He gritted his teeth to make that vision go away.  He wanted to remember her as she had been on those picnics they had both loved so well, down by the river.  How her dress and hair had shined brightly in the sun.  How wonderful the chicken had tasted.  That had been their last weekend together.  Damn it!!  He poked the fire again and remembered the deafening noise.  The entire line of Confederate artillery at Gettysburg, consisting of approximately 175 cannon, when they all concentrated their fire on Cemetery Ridge.  That shelling was deafening.  A surgeon had later told him that was why he was now nearly deaf at times.  When his heart beat fast and his breath shortened, usually when he or his men were under fire, all other sounds faded into the background.  It was as if his head was wrapped with a heavy woolen scarf.  Not totally silent, but heavily muffled.  His hearing would eventually return, usually one or two hours after things quieted down.

The major's mind turned to the squad's past missions, and how he and his four men now found themselves in camp just north of the Virginia-North Carolina border. It was still odd to see them in civilian clothes, and not their Confederate uniforms. But most of their missions in the last two years had been out of uniform. As drilling and training officer for the 35th Virginia Infantry regiment Ward had become known to high-ranking officers such as Brig. Gen. Albert G. Jenkins and later to Walter Taylor. Taylor was an adjutant to Gen. Robert E. Lee, overseeing the paperwork and administrative functions of the general's army. He signed Lee's general orders as "A.A.G.", which stood for Assistant Adjutant General. In late 1862, only 2 months after Helen's death, Ward had been entrusted with carrying a coded message through enemy lines to Richmond. He and Lieut. Peters (also of the 35th Virginia) had successfully delivered the coded dispatch to the Confederate War Department. It was a few months later that he was asked again to carry secret, coded messages between the army headquarters and the generals in the field. He was asked to choose a few men that could be trusted beyond the shadow of a doubt to relay orders and messages over many miles of Virginia countryside, usually at night. Lt. Peters would be his second in command. He and Peters then picked Sergeant Stephens and Private Thompson from another Virginia regiment. Stephens had uncanny night vision, which they could certainly use when they traveled at night. Private Thompson was an expert woodsman and could find trails and cowpaths that others seemed to overlook. They had next recruited Private Wells, who was an experienced scout and knew how to blend in with the woods.

On their first mission as a complete five man squad, they had been ordered to a small town in Ohio to warn a friend of the South who was the editor of a small town newspaper. The editor had been steadily sending funds (sometimes gold, sometimes currency,) and information south. Walter Taylor appeared to know where the newspaperman had obtained the gold, but never discussed it. Taylor had received word that someone in town was gathering evidence against the editor, and was about to have him captured and hung. The major and Lt. Peters had crossed the Ohio River and Sgt. Stephens had gone on ahead a day early. Once in town, Stephens surveyed the town and posted a small handbill in a conspicuous place on a pole. The handbill announced a horse auction in a neighboring town. The auction itself was unimportant, and in fact fictitious. What was important were the three numbers "130" penciled at the bottom of the handbill. The major recognized the code immediately. The first digit represented a point on the compass: 1 meant north, 2 meant east, 3 represented south, and so on. The next two digits were how many yards in that direction. Thus 130 would mean north, 30 yards (from the handbill's location.) At that point would be concealed a map or another message about where and when to meet. The major found the hidden message and met up with Stephens. They were able to warn the editor just in time for him to escape to another part of Ohio, where he was able to continue his undercover efforts. The man who had almost exposed the editor's mission conveniently committed suicide the next day.

Their second mission had taken place when Lee moved his army north into Pennsylvania in June and July of 1863. Lee sent Gen. Albert G. Jenkins and his cavalry brigade into Pennsylvania, early in June, with the idea of capturing the capitol of Harrisburg. Jenkins specifically requested that Ward and his squad be assigned on "detached duty" to Jenkins' cavalry. His excuse was that his best scouts from the 8th Virginia Cavalry had to be left behind in the Virginia Valley as a rear guard. The evening after Jenkins' Brigade crossed over into Pennsylvania, a courier arrived after dark with a message only for the eyes of Gen. Jenkins. The coded message revealed that an old friend of Jenkins was being held in the county jail at Chambersburg, on trumped up charges, and was to be hung in a few days. Jenkins thought up a plan of how to free his friend. Being a Harvard educated lawyer before the war, he wrote up a very convincing extradition order to have his friend taken from jail and turned over to a deputy, who would be Henry Ward. One of Jenkins' adjutants produced a U.S. Deputy Marshall's badge and handed it to Ward. Jenkins knew a county judge, and forged his signature to the order. If the paper was checked and the judge contacted, he would verify (and lie,) that he had signed the paper. At dawn the next day, Jenkins had dispatched Ward, Peters, and Stephens, who were able to bluff their way in and got the man out of jail. They delivered the grateful man to Gen. Jenkins.

Now their mission was to carry another coded message and packet of papers to Governor Harrison Lane of North Carolina at Raleigh. With the surrender of Gen. Lee and the Army of Northern Virginia, at Appomattox, Richmond was in an uproar. The city was partially evacuated on April 2, 1865, and Lee had surrendered a week later. President Jefferson Davis sent a message by courier to Ward's hotel in Richmond for him to hurry and meet with Davis at a stage stop south of town. The Confederate president was fleeing south with a guard detail. They met late in the evening, and it was at that meeting that Davis passed to Ward a leather pouch packed with papers. Davis explained how important it would be to the South to recover from what was coming. Ward realized later that Davis knew then that the end was near for the Confederacy. "Put these papers directly in the hands of Governor Harrison Lane at Raleigh. They are bearer bonds from England that will serve to recover not only the state of North Carolina, but hopefully help some of the other southern states," Davis had stated solemnly. He also mentioned that there was a set of parole papers for Ward and each of his men in the pouch. Ward thought of asking how those papers could be legal, since neither he nor any of his men had "taken the oath," or signed anything, but thought better of it. In a way Ward hoped this would indeed be their last mission.

The major poked the fire and again he saw the horse standing in the middle of the road with his head lowered, as if ashamed. He threw the stick in the fire and noticed dawn was breaking.

## Chapter 2

The group saddled their horses, loaded their pack horse, and broke camp. Thompson and Wells were sent on ahead to scout. The other three rode along in silence for the first couple of hours. They passed well-tended farms with several older men out working their fields. The farms gave way to a tree-lined road with forest on their left. As the trees became thicker on both sides of the road, the major signaled for a slow-down to a walk. Listening intently and on the alert for danger, the men heard a horse give a snort in the woods off to their right. This was followed by three riders slowly emerging from the trees on that side. They turned into the road directly facing the major's group, about 50 feet ahead. The three riders stopped abreast in the road. At that instant three more riders came into the road from the left. The six men, none in uniform, all lined up abreast and stopped in the road, blocking it. The major and his men slowly approached the six riders who also advanced slowly. As the two groups neared each other, the major sensed rather than saw Peters slowly move his hand over the butt of his pistol. He also knew that Stephens would be taking similar action. When the gap was narrowed to about twenty feet, both groups halted.

The leader of the six riders casually inquired, "Where you boys headed?"

The major answered, "Just headin' south."

The stranger said, "You boys ride like soldiers. Are you Rebs that have been paroled?"

The major answered, "Yep, we're just headin' to near Raleigh to visit friends."

The stranger asked, "Have you heard or seen any Yankee stragglers causin' problems on the way down here?"

The major truthfully answered, "Yeah, back up near Reedsville we heard the town folks talkin' about three stragglers tryin' to raid some houses and chicken coops, and things like that. We helped the townspeople go out and try to track them down, but they evidently escaped back north."

The stranger said, "If'n I was to ask my ol' friend Jim Waters up in Reedsville if he knew something about that, just what would he tell me?"

14

The major grinned and said, "Ol' Jim wouldn't tell you a thing, since he has another month or two to serve in the Grants Town jail, quite a distance away."

All the strangers snickered and chuckled. The major and his men had passed the test. The stranger ended the conversation with "You boys be careful now, and watch out for them Yankee stragglers." They then parted to the two sides of the road, giving an obvious signal that the major could pass.

With a sigh of relief, the squad continued down the road.

A few hours later, the squad neared the town of Falls Bluff. The major mentioned to the men that this was where they were to meet up with one of their contacts, nick-named Stonewall. The small town appeared quiet in the afternoon sun. There was a cluster of plain, clapboard houses on either side of the main street near the edge of town, surrounding a one-room school. On the left side of the street, after they passed the cluster of homes, was the church, the small post office, a doctor's office, a lawyer's office, the general store, where two men stood talking and smoking, a vacant boarded up building, and a small newspaper office. On the right side of the main street were the blacksmith's shop, where the blacksmith was beating out a horseshoe, the stable next door, a two-story hotel, a saloon, a small store, two other offices, and an old tavern.

In front of the general store was a hitching post with a hand-written sign tacked to it. The sign read: "The Stonewall Association will meet at 7pm," and at the bottom were the initials "B.C." The major immediately recognized one of their coded messages. He understood the reference to Stonewall and 7pm, but the "B.C." was new to him. As the others looked carefully over the town, the major pulled a small notebook from his jacket pocket. He leafed through a couple of pages and found the code. "B.C." was their code for "behind the church." So the seemingly innocent sign meant that their contact, Stonewall, would be behind the church at 7pm waiting for a meeting. Ward would have to locate Thompson and Wells before that. It was Thursday, April 13, 1865.

The men settled for a meager dinner at the local saloon, and killed time until the meeting. At a few minutes before seven, Major Ward and Lt. Peters walked to the church, leaving Sgt. Stephens at the corner to stand lookout. The hour came and went with no one appearing. At 7:30, Ward knew that there was not going to be a meeting, and the three men met and decided to stay overnight and figure out a new plan. As they walked up the block from the church, Ward noticed a light on in the small newspaper office. The clapboard sign over the door declared it to be the home of the "Falls Bluff Weekly." As the major approached the newspaper office, he noted on the window that the weekly paper was "Published each Friday."

Ward exclaimed: "What a lucky break!"

## Chapter 3

The "lucky break" was that an alternative method of posting a coded message was through a local newspaper. No doubt the lighted office meant that the editor was setting type to print the paper the next day. Ward tried the door knob of the office, and it was locked, of course. He tapped lightly on the glass, and a shadowy figure approached and opened the door just a crack.

A woman's voice said "I'm sorry, we're closed."

Ward said, "I was hoping it wasn't too late to put in a last-minute ad."

The woman replied, "I do have a couple of blank spaces left. Come on in."

As Ward and Peters stepped through the door, the shadowy woman moved to a table and turned up an oil lamp. She picked up a couple of scrap pieces of paper to write down what the major wanted in the ad. When she turned around to face the major she walked forward and extended her hand. The major's hearing went out, and a loud hum filled his brain. For an instant he was frozen in his tracks. It wasn't her face so much as her eyes. They had the same deep look as Helen's. They were that light blue, like Helen's. His feelings in an instant ran from remembrance, to grief, to excitement. His heart raced. After what seemed to him like hours, but was really only seconds, his senses returned, and his hearing came back.

She was still extending her hand, and saying "My name is Ardelia Simmons, my friends call me "Delia."

The major took the extended hand, which felt warm and firm. He managed to blurt out: "I'm Henry Ward, and this here's Drew Peters."

He took one deep breath, and stated, "We would like to speak to your husband about placing a short ad."

Delia responded, "My husband is dead. He was killed at the battle of Cloyd's Mountain in '64. He left me to run the newspaper, so I'm afraid you're stuck with me."

Ward stammered and said, "I'm sorry, I didn't mean any disrespect. What unit was your husband in?"

Delia responded, "The 45th. Virginia, under Col. Browne. "

17

Ward added, "I knew several men of the 45th. They were a courageous bunch. Then he quickly added, to Peters's shock: "We belong to the 35th Virginia, and are on a secret mission to Raleigh."

Peters gave a short gasp at Ward's revelation of a large part of their mission to this woman they didn't even know.

Delia smiled and replied: "I'm not surprised. I suspected something like that. The way you are dressed and armed. Hardly any of the men around here have a gun anymore. Your secret is safe with me." She paused then asked "Now what do you want in your ad? I have a newspaper to print."

Ward spoke slowly as Delia wrote, "Stonewall Association meeting postponed. Watch this NEWSPAPER B9." This would convey to their contact that they would try again to meet Friday night at 9 o'clock, and the "NEWSPAPER B9" meant behind the newspaper building.

Peters pulled Ward aside and expressed his concern about waiting another 24 hours, stuck in town and not able to move further south toward their destination.

Ward's thoughtful response was: "What are our options? This person is supposed to have important information about the route from here to Raleigh. If he's a no-show then we can pack up and move out tomorrow night."

For lack of a better plan, Peters shrugged, sighed, and responded, "if you're sure."

Delia approached the two men and said: "It's all set. The ad will be on the back page of tomorrow's paper. That'll be a dollar, in U.S money if you have it." Ward produced the money and handed it to her. He had been careful before he left Richmond to be sure and obtain from Walter Taylor several dollars of U.S. currency, and a few dollars in Confederate bills.

As the men walked in silence back to the hotel, at nine p.m., each was trying hard to think of a smarter way to proceed if things fell apart in Falls Bluff. When they reached the old hotel, Peters and Stephens fell onto the bed, and Ward threw an extra blanket on the floor, with the saddlebags holding the valuable documents that they were carrying. Ward had met up with Thompson and Wells, and they decided to stay with the horses in the stable. After an hour of lying there wide awake, Ward shook Peters and told him "I'm going back to the newspaper to help Delia get the paper out."

Peters grunted "okay" and rolled over. Ward slipped on his boots and shoved the Remington .44 into his belt and headed out the door.

Ward arrived at the newspaper office, and tapped lightly on the door. Delia carefully opened the door a small crack. She firmly said "Go away, we're closed!"

Ward said calmly, "Just your new press man reporting for duty, ma'am."

"It's about time. I need some help," Delia declared, as she swung open the door.

Ward quickly added, "I worked for a few months at the *Weekly Crescent* in New Orleans before the war, and saw how much work is involved in getting the paper out." Ward rolled up his sleeves as he inquired: "Where are we and are we ready to print?"

"Almost. I need another vat of ink from the back storeroom."

"Just point me to the door and I'll fetch it." Ward stated.

After retrieving the ink, they moved a stack of the blank newsprint over to the press, on an old wooden cart. After inking the set type, the monotonous, repetitive work began of placing a blank newsprint page on the press and turning the arm down to push it against the inked type slugs. Then that page was pulled out, and another inserted and printed.

During the long night, the two exchanged remembrances about growing up and funny little stories about their early lives. They found they had in common some funny and strange relatives, as do all families. Neither of them had children. They also shared the common tragedy of losing their spouse in a violent manner. A long silence followed the sharing as both remembered their times with their loved one. Dawn came quickly as the printing progressed to the last page.

After Ward returned with the cart of blank newsprint from the storeroom, he told Delia, "I don't see any more stacks of newsprint back there? Is that all you have?"

She replied, "That's it. It has been getting harder and harder to order newsprint paper in the last year. I'm also getting low on ink. So we have enough of both to finish this edition, but I don't know how we will produce another paper for a while."

After another few hours of operating the press and Delia folding the papers, they declared the edition finished at 10 a.m. Delia went two doors down to the general store to borrow young Jimmy, who was her newspaper distribution person. He would also take a cart load to the front porch of the hotel, where the stagecoach stopped around noon.

Ward went back to the hotel for a bath and a few hours sleep. If Stonewall read and deciphered their coded ad, then they would try again to meet at nine that night. Peters and Stephens were already up and went out to meet with Thompson and Wells to see if they had heard any news. They would also check on the horses at the stable.

At dinner that night, the only news of value was that Thompson had heard from another man traveling up from the south, that a Union Army company was in the area south of town.

Night finally came, and as the streets grew dark, Ward and Peters laid out the plan. Ward ordered: "Peters and I will go for the meeting with Stonewall. Stephens, you stand guard in the shadows at the front of the newspaper building and watch the main street. Thompson and Wells, I want you at the stable with the horses saddled and ready to go. If this meeting doesn't come about, we need to leave town tonight, and quickly. We will have to assume that Stonewall was caught or got scared, and probably for a good reason."

At a few minutes before nine Ward and Peters took their positions behind the newspaper building, with Stephens at the front of the building in the shadows. At nine o'clock, a light appeared at one end of the alley, and then another light at the other end. As the men watched from the shadows, it became clearer that each man had a light and what appeared to be a shotgun, and both were moving slowly down the alley from each end, toward where Peters and Ward were waiting in the shadows.

Peters whispered, "This doesn't look good. I think we're trapped in the middle."

Ward whispered, "You said it."

As both men drew their pistols and tried to decide their next action, a small gust of warm air engulfed the two men, as a back door opened just behind them.

Delia's low voice urged, "Quick, in here!"

The two men hesitated then saw that was indeed the best course of action, and ducked inside the back door of the newspaper office. With a very dim kerosene lamp, shaded by her hand, Delia led the men into the back storeroom and to another door in the side of the building. She opened that door and led them into what appeared to be a vacant back room in the building next door to the newspaper office. Ward heard a rustling and a cough, and drew his Remington, as Peters drew his pistol.

Stephens came into the dim light and whispered: "It's me, major, Delia found me and drug me in here...fortunately." After a pause he added, "Major, meet Stonewall."

Coming into the light was a short, teenage boy with a tousled head of black hair.

Startled, Ward remarked, "He's just a kid!"

Stephens returned, "He is a very smart kid, and you need to hear what he has to say."

Delia added, "I know this boy and he is very smart and observant. I guessed he might have been your contact, so I pulled him in when I saw the two no-goods heading for the alley."

Stonewall came forward, "Sir, I'm sorry I didn't make the meeting last night, but there were rumors all over town about the two gunmen in the black coats that you saw in the alley. I was afraid they were Pinkertons, and had come to kill me." Ward nodded his understanding.

It was actually a year previous that Stonewall had been recruited. When Pvt. Wells had been on a rare furlough to visit a sick parent across the state line in North Carolina, while heading back to Virginia on his return to his unit, he had stayed overnight at the house of Stonewall and his family. Their last name was Phillips. Wells determined that the families' sympathies were definitely with the South. Even though they already had one son in the Virginia infantry, they appeared anxious to help in other ways. Wells observed that Stonewall was indeed an intelligent boy, so he taught the boy the code system that the major carried in his notebook. They discussed it like a game boys might play. While Wells did not give the boy the whole system, he gave him enough to interpret a few codes, which was now paying off.

Stonewall let out a sigh of relief and continued, "Major, for the last few days I have been able to roam around outside of town on the South road. But your man heard right, there's a company of Rhode Island infantry blocking the South road about two miles outside of town."

Ward immediately questioned him, "What are they doing here? I can't believe the Virginia troops haven't rousted them."

Stonewall replied, "They are still looking for President Davis, and are expecting his carriage and guard to come down this way and try to escape south on that road."

Ward asked, "How did you get this information out of them?"

Stonewall grinned, "I just mess my hair up some, and rub a little dirt on my face and take on my 'orphan look' as my mother calls it. I acted like I was poor and hungry, and they let me share a cup of beans. Within fifteen minutes, they just ignored me and a few across from me was talkin.' They said as how the war was practically over now. Is that true?"

"I'm afraid so, son. Lee's surrendered and Richmond has been evacuated. I don't see how they can hold out much longer," Ward stated with a sigh.

Ward thought for a minute and then asked Stephens and Peters "What are our options? Is there another road out of here South?"

Stonewall and Delia both answered in unison, "No."

After another pondering moment, Peters offered, "We could just mosey up and try to bluff our way through, not all five of us together, but one or two at a time, split up."

Ward countered, "Too risky. They probably would search our saddlebags, and that would be the end of that."

Delia volunteered, "There is another way. There is a little-known cowpath just outside the edge of town that goes over around the base of the mountain and comes out four or five miles south, which should get you clear of the Yank company. Stonewall, I know your real name and you live just outside of town. Just before the Atkins farm there are two beech trees just to the left side of the road. Just next to those two beeches is a cowpath going off to the west."

Stonewall added, "I know where that is, but nobody uses it."

Ward said, "Sounds like just what we need."

Stephens asked the next obvious question, "Do we leave now or wait until dawn?"

Both Wells and Thompson, the two scouts and trackers interjected, "If we leave an hour before dawn, we can be off the main road, and onto the cowpath before daylight."

Delia added, "That sounds like the right plan, the two or three small farms you pass before the cowpath are owned by good loyal Virginians whom I know well, and they wouldn't turn you in to the Yanks, if their lives depended on it."

Ward made one more statement before the group, "Stonewall, thank you so much for your help. Stay safe." They shook hands, and Stonewall slipped quietly out the front door of the empty building.

Ward then turned and said, "Since we don't know who those two with shotguns were in the alley, let's get our things from the hotel and move to the stable, and catch a few hours sleep, and take turns standing guard. That way, if we have to leave early, we'll be prepared."

The men agreed, and slipped out the front of the empty building, one at a time.

Ward turned to Delia, and said, "Thank you for bailing us out, and all the help. Maybe I can return the favor when all this madness is over."

Delia smiled and said, "I look forward to it."

They shook hands, a little longer than required, and Ward was gone into the night.

None of the little group who had met so briefly had any inkling of what had happened that evening, hundreds of miles away, in a place called Ford's Theater in Washington.

An American Indian travois.

## Chapter 4

The major yawned and stretched as he got up from his bed of hay in the stable and stumbled to the back door in the dim pre-dawn light. Thompson was leaning against the door frame, standing guard. Wells was guarding the front door on the other side of the stable. Ward squinted at his pocket watch in the moonlight; it was 5:30 in the morning. He asked Thompson, "All quiet?"

Thompson replied, "All quiet, major, not a peep."

"Get the others up, we need to get going," ordered the major.

Thompson walked back into the stable where the other two were still asleep. He nudged them with his toe, saying gruffly, "Get up, you sleepy-heads, time to rise and shine!"

The horses had been mostly packed and saddled the night before, and only required a few minutes of checking cinches and straps, and tying on of bedrolls. Ward instructed each man to check and make sure his weapons were loaded and ready. Just as they headed out the back door of the stable, a figure appeared out of the shadows, leading a small mule. It was Stonewall.

"What the hell are you doing here?" grumbled the major.

"I got to thinkin' that you guys might have a hard time finding them two beech trees, where the cow path starts, so I thought I'd guide you that far," answered Stonewall.

"I see you're determined to do this, so mount up and you and I will ride in front," ordered the major. He added: "Thompson and Wells, you two in back to watch our rear. Take turns leading the pack horse." The little procession headed slowly and quietly out of the stable, into the alley, and one block down they turned onto the road heading south out of town. There were no lights burning in any of the last few buildings as they reached the edge of town. A lone mongrel dog limped slowly across in front of them.

The squad rode along slowly and as quietly as possible when they came to the first of the farms along the road. There was a light burning in the kitchen of the first farmhouse, but no one was outside. A short distance later they rode by the second farm. One old man and a young boy were carrying buckets of water to a barn. The two were barely visible in the waning moonlight. They stopped and stared at the group as it passed. Ward tipped his hat to the gentleman, and to his surprise, the old gentleman straightened up, and stiffly saluted. Ward looked back and realized that the six with the pack horse did look a little too much like an army squad. They were riding as three pairs closely together, with the pack horse trailing behind. Ward ordered everyone to spread out a little more, so as not to look like a small army. The last farm before the cow path was dark and appeared abandoned. Dawn was breaking.

About a mile later, Stonewall said, "Here's the turn off to the cow path. This is as far as I go."

Ward again thanked him for all his help, bid him to stay safe, and added, "Maybe we will meet again when this is over."

Before Stonewall turned his little mule around and headed home, he suddenly added: "I just remembered something that might help you. My daddy told me that when he traveled the cow path once, he and his brother had found shelter in a cave that was about half way in. He said there was a small clearing on the right, in front of the cave, where the horses could be tied. Good luck, major!" And with a tip of his little cap, the boy headed back toward town.

As the squad turned off the main road, the path narrowed immediately. The group proceeded in single file, with the major in the lead. In a few hundred feet, the path went into the woods, and as the trees closed in on each side of the trail, the men had to slow down to clear a few over-hanging branches. The major and Peters each used their Bowie knives; the major hacking limbs on the left and Peters the limbs on the right. After a few hundred yards of this very slow travel, the trees cleared and became more separated, which greatly eased their movement.

After another two or three hours of slow travel, a narrow, fast-running stream appeared on their left. A few hundred feet later, the stream actually crossed over the cow path. With a small clearing across the path and stream, probably where cattle had stopped to drink in years past, the major called a halt for rest and to water the horses and fill their canteens. Having not been able to get breakfast, the men dug through their packs and saddle-bags and produced some beef jerky, a couple of biscuits they had taken from the saloon, and other pieces of food that didn't require cooking.

With a brief repast, the men tightened their horses' cinches and saddles and mounted up to move down the trail. The major ordered: "Stephens, you out in front and keep a sharp watch. I'll take the rear guard for a while to watch our back trail." With that, the men moved out in single file.

After about an hour of silent travel, a commotion occurred in the front where Stephens was. In an instant it happened. Stephen's horse bucked and whinnied, rearing and pawing in the air and throwing Stephens to the ground. A loud grunt issued and an instant later, a single "boom" from Stephens' LeMat pistol. Ward rode quickly to the front, in time to see Stephens lying on his back with his pistol pointed ahead of him. There lay a large timber rattlesnake with its head blown off from the shotgun charge of the LeMat. The large snake had been coiled in the middle of the path, producing a loud rattle that frightened the horse, resulting in its rider being thrown. Fortunately Stephen had killed the snake before it could strike. Unfortunately, Stephens was gritting his teeth in a large degree of pain.

"Major, I think I broke something," the injured Stephens uttered.

Peters and Ward dismounted and knelt beside the injured man. Stephens said through clinched teeth, "It's my left leg."

As they looked at the leg, they could see a bulge between the knee and the thigh that was certainly unnatural. Peters took his Bowie knife and slit the pants leg. It was obvious that the bone was broken, and almost pushed through the skin.

"You won't be walking on that one for a while, Lige," the major commented. Peters said, "I'm afraid we are goin' to have to set it. I saw this done several times when I was in a field hospital after a battle. Which one of you has a pint of whiskey in his bag?" Thompson and Wells both looked sheepishly at each other, but Wells reluctantly reached into his saddle bag and produced the bottle. Peters handed it to Stephens, and said "Take a few swigs, you're going to need it."

He continued, "Major, go up to his head and you and Thompson grab under his arms to hold his upper body perfectly still. Lige, here's a piece of leather to bite on. This is going to hurt!" Peters knelt at Stephens's feet and got a firm grip on his ankle. He asked Ward and Thompson if they had a firm grip, to which they nodded. Peters said, "Ready… one-two-three!" On three, Peters pulled the ankle quickly. Stephens let out a long grunt of pain, but the large bump on the leg went down. Stephens breathed loudly for a few seconds, as the men relaxed. Peters felt carefully up the leg between the knee and the thigh, and declared, "I think we did the best we could. It feels like we got it pulled back together, pretty much."

Peters instructed the others, "We need to make a splint as long as his leg. Wells and Thompson go and cut us a pole. If you can find one four or five inches wide that we can split straight that would be best. Major, see if you can find an old shirt or underwear that we can tear some strips from."

The three went off on their assigned errands, and returned in a few minutes with a straight pole and some cloth strips. They placed the splint along the outside of Stephens' leg and tied it in four places with the cloth strips.

After a few minutes, Stephens seemed to settle down as the whiskey took effect, and he became quiet.

Ward remarked, "Let's hope no one else heard that gunshot."

As the others stood looking down at Stephens, Ward said "I think we need to build a travois, like the Indians use." The others looked at him with blank looks.

The major explained: "The travois was a drag sled that has been around for decades in North America. It has been used in various forms by the North American Indians when moving from one area to another. It consisted of two long poles, tied together, with at least one cross-piece, resembling a long, stretched "H." Originally it was probably developed to move a teepee, and used the long poles from it as part of the travois. With extra cross-pieces, a heavier load or even an ill person can be hauled. Each of the two side poles were tied on either side of a horse, and the other end of the poles rested on the ground."

After the major explained this to the men, he sent them again into the woods: "Cut two long poles for the sides, long enough to hold him and fit on either side of the horse. Then cut four or five short pieces, to serve as cross pieces. Peters, you and I will go through the saddle bags and supplies on the pack horse, to find a rope, leather straps, or more pieces of clothing we can tear into strips to tie this drag sled together." Ward and Peters hunted through their supplies on the pack horse, finally locating a long piece of thin rope, which they could use to tie the frame together. Ward also took one of their blankets and folded it to make a pad for the sled. After securely tying the sled together, next came the question of which horse to use with the travois: Stephens' horse or the pack horse. Stephens suggested, "Better hook it to the pack horse, mine is always skittish about changing loads." So with Stephens saying soothing things to his horse, they transferred two bags of supplies onto his horse, and tied the travois onto the pack horse. Finally with Stephens on the sled, they were ready to move out. The cow path was a little wider for some distance, which made things easier. Thompson and Wells brought up the rear, to keep an eye on Stephens.

At the slow rate of travel they felt was necessary to keep from jostling Stephens, the squad could only manage a slow walk. After keeping a steady, if slow, pace the squad paused to let the horses drink from the stream in mid-afternoon. Thompson moved his horse so he was close beside Ward at the stream. He whispered casually to Ward, "Major, there's someone in the woods on our right. He is alone, and he has been following us I think since we started out with the sled. When we pull out, I'll drop back as if to watch Stephens, and slip into the woods behind him, and see if I can get the drop on him."

Ward nodded slightly, and as the men finished watering their horses, he turned back to the cow path, and casually straightened his hat brim. The men stiffened, recognizing Ward's signal to "Look out, stay alert, something's up." Thompson slowly walked with his horse back to give Stephens a drink from his canteen. He dropped back several feet, and disappeared into the woods. They formed their line again, with Ward and Peters in the front. Ward had his Remington laying in his lap, and Peters with his rifle across his lap. They only went a few hundred yards, when a ragtag, disheveled man fell out of the woods into the middle of the road. Thompson followed, with his Colt revolver pointed at the fallen man's head. He exclaimed: "Well, looky what I found sneaking around in the woods!" The man sat up and dusted himself off, and only then did the squad see that he had on a blue, U.S. Army jacket. Ward and Wells both rode forward and also pointed their pistols at the man. He was within seconds of dying in a hail of bullets.

Ward said, "Looks like we have ourselves a Yankee straggler." As soon as he had said it, Wells rode forward with his shotgun cocked and pointed at the man. He was obviously ready to kill him in an instant. Ward said in his officer's voice, "Hold your fire! Everybody ease off, he's unarmed."

Ward holstered his pistol and rode forward, until he was directly over the man. He said, "Looks like you've got about ten seconds before someone here shoots you just for wearing a blue jacket…TALK!"

The straggler asked, "Is it alright if I stand?"

Ward replied, "Get up slowly and keep your hands in plain sight."

The man rose slowly, holding his hands in plain view. Looking directly at the major, he said, "I'm Private Rosen. I was conscripted into the 14th Rhode Island U. S. Infantry, six months ago. That's the regiment that is guarding the main road. I am one of three Jews conscripted into Company C." He grinned and went on to say, "Unfortunately our choice of officers wasn't the best. The three of us were given the worst duty

29

possible, and shown that obviously we were lower than negroes. One of the others reported our sergeant, who was the main instigator of our troubles. Two nights later, the one who reported was beaten within an inch of his life. When we went into camp two nights ago, I overheard talk that after the next skirmish, there might be three less Jews in the company. We were scared for our lives, so we skipped in the middle of the night, and went our separate ways. I've been hiding in the woods ever since. So if you're going to shoot me, just get it over with."

Deadly silence enveloped the group, with only a single bird chirping in the deep woods.

In a few very long seconds, Rosen added, "Judging by your horses and weapons, I don't think you're Yanks. Are you maybe some Johnny Rebs who were paroled at Appomattox?"

Wells said to the major, "He's figured us out, we've got to kill him, or he'll tell everyone who and where we are."

After two seconds of thought, the major said, "Back off, private, I've got another plan for him. Let's tie him up on Stephens' horse and take him along. At least until we hit the main road. We may need to use him as a bargaining chip if we get stopped by a Yank patrol."

The major turned to Rosen and said, "Private Rosen, looks like you get to live a few more days, providing you agree to go along with us peaceably, and don't try to escape. If you do try to escape we will have to shoot you. And to answer your question, we are indeed ex-Confederates who were paroled. We're heading south into North Carolina to visit some old friends. If we get stopped, you go along with that story. Got it?"

Rosen answered, "Got it clear...sir."

Peters proceeded to use their last piece of thin rope and tied Rosen's hands together in front of him. He helped him up on Stephens' horse, then tied his hands to the pommel, with the end of the rope.

In a few minutes, the growing party of six men moved out again on the cow path. The next three or four hours passed without incident. As the shadows began to lengthen into early evening, the air took on a cooler feel, and a slow drizzle of rain began to fall. The major called a halt just long enough for Peters to get an old oil skin from his bedroll, and to go back and cover up Stephens. Peters smiled and remarked to Stephens, "We can't have you catching the consumption after all you've been through, now can we?" Stephens was able to manage a grin.

After another hour of slow travel in the drizzling rain, Ward finally spotted the cave that Stonewall had mentioned as being about halfway in on the cow path. There indeed was a small clearing below the cave where they stopped and dismounted. Ward and Peters went up the small rise to investigate the size of the cave. To their surprise, it was large enough for all six men to easily get inside, with room for a small campfire. Ward said, "Thompson and Wells gather some firewood, all dead limbs from standing trees, if possible. We can chance a fire back in the back of the cave, which shouldn't be visible from the path." Peters untied their prisoner from the horse, and marched him at gunpoint up to the cave. The horses were tied up to trees and given water, as they grazed on what grass was left in the clearing.

Ward approached Rosen and said sternly, "Here's where I go out on a limb. If I have your word as a gentleman that you won't try to jump one of us or try to escape, I will untie your hands. But understand, one of us will be at the mouth of the cave at all times, with orders to shoot you if you try to run. Do I have your word?"

Rosen answered, "You have my word, sir. And by the way, what do I call you? By how you address and order these men, you are obviously a ranking officer."

Ward answered, "Just call me Henry or Mr. Ward. And this fellow here is Drew Peters. That's all you need to know."

The fire was soon crackling in the back of the cave. Some of the men took off their wet jackets or pants, and laid them on rocks to dry in front of the fire. Fixing a meal was the next challenge. Two of the men were looking at Rosen and grumbling, presumably not wanting to share their food with a prisoner of war. Ward saw the looks and quickly informed the group that all six would share the food equally. That stopped the grumbling. Peters and Wells did the honors, and made do well with what they had. They still had some of their slab of bacon, which Peters carved into small chunks. After Wells gathered a small pot full of water, they threw in the last of their beans and added the chunks of bacon. As that cooked, they put on their small coffee pot with enough water for six people. Fortunately, three days ago, Thompson had traded a large tobacco plug for a small bag of coffee. It would not be very strong coffee. Meanwhile, Ward produced three biscuits that Delia had contributed before they had left town, which he cut into six equal pieces. Wells revealed that he had picked up two apples from the last farmer's tree just outside of Falls Bluff. So each man got a small apple slice. Wells took a small plate of food to Stephens, helped him sit upright and he ate with relish. Rosen was then fed from the same plate, partly filled with the last of the bean-bacon delight, his half of a biscuit, and one slice of apple. He said "Much appreciated," to Wells, who simply grunted. After the meal, Thompson and Wells took the plates, bucket, and pot to the stream and washed everything. On their way to the stream, they fed the last of their hardtack and other scraps to the horses.

Eventually things got quiet, as the men settled down and stared into the fire, happy with their bellies full of the first hot food they had had in days. Ward turned to their prisoner and said, "Well, Rosen, the five of us know our stories and how we ended up here, but how about you…what's your story?"

The man cleared his throat and started out, "Well, as I told you back at our meeting in the middle of the road I was conscripted into the 14th Rhode Island Infantry last year."

Thompson interrupted and asked, "Wait a minute, all we have ever heard was that the evil Confederates were the only ones who drafted men off their farms. The North drafted also?"

"They certainly did," Rosen answered. "My family lived along the Wood River in southern Rhode Island. It was a good, swift-running little river most of the year, and my family had a combined grist mill and sawmill that we ran. My father passed away in 1859, and my mother and I ran the mill, with the help of two neighborhood Jewish men. Last fall, this Union Army company came through the small towns in the bottom of the state, and conscripted the three of us, even though I complained about what would become of my mother. They mounted us on horses at gunpoint and we were taken to a camp in New York, even though we were promised that we would not have to leave our state. From there we ended up in Virginia early this year. My mother has gone to live with her sister in Connecticut, and when she left Rhode Island, she took my six year old brother with her, and I really miss seeing him. If the war really is almost over, I sure hope I can make it home, bring my mother and brother home, and we can return to our happy life as it was before this darn war."

Ward's men all chimed in to say that they sure agreed with Rosen about that. Peters added, "We all feel that way. We five here have served our army and our country as best we could, and now we are just dreaming of getting back home."

After that exchange, things got quiet again. Someone had found an old pine knot that was crackling on the fire. Wells was yawning. Stephens was already asleep under his blanket. In the last few minutes it had become completely dark outside.

Ward said, "I'll take the first watch. Peters, I'll wake you at midnight. And you can wake Thompson early in the morning. Remember you are not only watching the path but also guarding a prisoner." The others rolled up in their blankets and fell into the good sleep.

No one came along the cow path during the night. The only noises were made by a few animals in the woods, and the crackling of the fire.

Ward came in close enough to the fire to see his watch and it was a few minutes before midnight. He shook Peters who woke immediately. He asked, "Is it my turn already?"

Ward answered, "'fraid so," and he handed Peters his loaded Remington.

Peters stretched, and walked to the cave mouth. On his way he checked Stephens and Rosen, who were both sound asleep.

Ward headed back to the campfire and threw another piece of wood on the fire, where the pine knot was still glowing. He stretched out on his bedroll, and immediately fell asleep.

Ward woke up, without knowing why. It was still dark outside the cave. Then he heard what had probably woke him up: a low moan. He sat up and listened. There it was again. He crawled over to where Stephens was, and discovered the source of the moan. Stephens was evidently in pain. Ward shook him gently and asked, "Lige, are you all right?"

Stephens answered, "It's just the way I am laying. Help me put my folded jacket under this hip." Ward grabbed the jacket, and he and Stephens stuffed it under the hip of the leg that was broken. Stephens replied "That's much better."

Ward went back closer to the fire to look at his watch. It was 5:30 and still dark. No use in waking the others up just yet. He put another stick on the fire, and stared into the sparks going up to the top of the cave. Then he thought: *That's funny.* It was odd that he wasn't thinking of Helen lying in the middle of the road, with the old horse holding its head down. He was thinking of himself and Delia inking the newspaper press back in Falls Bluff. He smiled. It was a good memory.

# Chapter 5

Capt. E. William Reynolds of the Pennsylvania Mounted Militia, IV Corps, U.S. Army, was not happy.  He and his company had just received word from their colonel that they would not be going home anytime soon.  Lee had surrendered, it was true, but there were still large divisions of Confederate armies in the field, and skirmishes still ongoing.  His company was stuck on the main road just south of the North Carolina-Virginia state line.  They were acting as a rear reserve guard to the 14th Rhode Island Infantry that was blocking the main road north, hoping to trap Jefferson Davis if he came their way.  Reynolds had just received an order that he was to mount a patrol with three days rations and be ready to ride at dawn.  There had been a report from a local informant of a band of Confederates that was on the old cow path and avoiding the 14th Rhode Island and would be coming back out on the main road.  Reynolds and his squad were to head up the cow path and try to intercept the guerillas. Reynolds and his colonel had a disagreement on the size of the squad, if it was to be five men or eight.  The colonel said five was enough. The captain sent for his best officer, Sergeant Homer Steinholtz, who had been with the captain since they had left Pennsylvania.  The Sergeant picked three privates that he knew to be good shots and were at home in the woods.  As they saddled their horses and checked their bags of provisions, no one talked.  All were as unhappy as the captain.  They had gone only a few hundred yards on the path, when they flushed out a straggler from the 14th Rhode Island who had been hiding in the woods.  He told an unlikely story of he and other Jews being mistreated by their sergeant, and pointed to that as the cause for his desertion. Steinholtz dispatched one of the privates to lead him on a rope back to their camp. Reynolds waited for a few hours while the private convinced the lieutenant to send two men back with the private, to join Reynold's squad so he would have a squad of seven. (This change was executed without the colonel's approval.) With all seven men present and ready, the captain gave the order to "move out." The patrol headed in single file back into the forest. A few hours in, the group came across a mangy looking gray horse, standing by the creek, with no saddle or brand.  They debated over whether to just shoot it, but the captain ordered them to put a rope around its neck and bring it along. If one of their good horses pulled up lame, it might come in handy.

Major Ward woke the men in the cave and they began repacking the horses. Their meager breakfast consisted of a weak pot of coffee and the last few pieces of leftover hardtack and biscuits. Next came the careful positioning of Stephens onto the travois, and the lashing of the sled again to the pack horse. Peters tied Rosen's hands in front of him and helped him onto Stephens's horse. With Ward on Andy in the lead, the squad headed out on the path a little after dawn. After two hours of slow travel, the path widened somewhat as they came to a large boulder the size of a small cabin. The path curved around the boulder, which blocked the men's view of the path ahead. When they rounded the boulder, with Ward in front, they came to an immediate halt. Facing Major Henry Stuart Ward, of the 35th Virginia Infantry, CSA, was Captain E. William Reynolds of the Pennsylvania Mounted Militia, USA, and his squad. The two men were only about fifteen feet apart, staring each other in the eyes. That moment of shock and silence seemed to all the men to have lasted an eternity, but was really only a few seconds. The men on both sides then took the obvious next step of starting to reach for their guns. Ward recovered from the shock quicker than anyone on his side, as did Reynolds.

Ward touched the brim of his hat, smiled, and said a cheery "Good morning, captain."

The response from Reynolds was a little tentative, "And good morning to you, sir."

After this exchange between the two officers, without a resulting volley of gunfire, Ward slowly shifted his hand away from his pistol, and put it straight down, pointing to the ground. Peters saw and understood this gesture of "ease off, men, hands off guns," and passed it to the others. Reynolds, in turn, gave his men a signal to relax, even if only slightly. Reynolds brought his horse slowly forward a couple of feet, without every taking his eyes from Ward's. Ward responded in like manner, bringing the two officers closer together. Reynolds' first question was the logical one of, "What are you boys doing on this little mountain path, and not on the main road?"

Ward explained, "We're paroled Confederate soldiers traveling to a small town near Raleigh, to stay with an old friend, and to be honest, captain, we heard while passing through Falls Bluff, just across in

Virginia, that the Union outfit blocking the main road was not likely to let us pass, alive."

Reynolds relaxed somewhat in his saddle, and smiled. He remarked, "That Rhode Island regiment does have somewhat of a reputation of shooting first, and asking questions later over the dead bodies." A snicker came from two of the Union soldiers, who received a dirty look backwards from the captain. He said, "Judging from your clothes and weapons, I don't take you boys to be scavengers or stray bushwhackers." He continued, in a casual manner, "I don't reckon you gentlemen have any parole papers on you, do you?"

Ward smiled and stated, "As a matter of fact, we do, captain." He continued, "I am going to reach slowly into my coat and come out with only a leather wallet with papers in it." He paused, making sure not to move too quickly.

Sergeant Steinholtz, on his horse just a few feet behind his captain, put his hand on his revolver. Reynolds knew his sergeant well, and turned slightly, saying, "Relax, sergeant, we're doing just fine up here."

With that remark, Ward moved his hand slowly into his coat, without taking his eyes off of Reynolds, and slowly pulled out his large leather wallet. He opened the wallet, and extracted five folded papers. He eased his horse forward the remaining few feet, until he could extend his hand and pass the papers to Reynolds. He was sweating a little, hoping the forged documents would pass the test.

Reynolds accepted the papers, and opened the first. He inquired, "Sergeant Peters, is this your true parole and your oath, and is this your signature?"

Ward swallowed hard. The rank was wrong on Peters' forged papers! He was a lieutenant, not a sergeant. If Peters got peeved and said something without thinking, they may all be dead men.

Peters answered firmly, "Yes, sir, it is."

Reynolds next asked the same question of each of the other men, and received the same affirmative answer. He rode slowly past Ward to where Stephens was on the sled, and asked him the same question.

Stephens answered, "Yes sir, it is my oath and my signature."

Reynolds returned to face Ward and asked, "The date is a little smeared on some of these papers, what day were you paroled?"

Ward answered, "It was April 10, the day after Lee's surrender."

Reynolds pondered it for a few seconds, then extended the papers back to Ward, stating, "I guess they are real, Major Ward."

Ward locked Reynolds in the eye, and without blinking, said "I assure you, sir, they are."

Reynolds now changed his expression to one of curiosity, and looking at Rosen, asking, "It looks to me like you have a prisoner, in a blue uniform. Exactly what are you doing with him?"

Ward said, "He's Private Rosen, of the 14th Rhode Island. We found him sneaking through the woods, alongside of us, so we adopted him."

Snickers again from the Union soldiers.

Ward continued, "He told us a story of how he and two others had been mistreated, and when it was reported, one of them was beaten severely, so he and his buddies skedaddled. Since to us he's just another mouth to feed, we'd like to turn him over to you, with the request that you listen to his story, before you stand him up and shoot him for desertion."

Reynolds replied, "As a matter of fact, we came across another deserter with a similar story, earlier today, back near the junction with the main road. To be honest, we're not interested in staging a court-martial and shooting him. Our unit has lost several men due to diseases, and we may be able to take him in as a transfer, and work out the paperwork later. Private Rosen, do you agree with that arrangement?"

The prisoner answered, immediately, "Yes, sir, I do!"

With that, Peters took the reins of Stephen's horse and led it up to beside Ward. Ward said, "That's a good horse and we'd like to keep it, if possible."

Reynolds turned to his sergeant, and said, "Sergeant, take a walk around all these gentlemen's horses and check for a 'U.S.' brand. If you find any, we'll be taking those horses."

With a reply of "Yessir, captain," Steinholtz started his horse slowly around Ward's squad, checking the flanks of each horse for a brand. He returned to Captain Reynolds and reported, "No brands on any of them, sir."

Reynolds again addressed Ward, and said, "Tell you what we'll do. We'll do some horse trading. We'll take Rosen on the horse he's on, and we'll give you this old gray we found along the trail." He paused to see if that was going to cause an argument.

Ward only thought a second before replying, "Yes, sir, that's a good trade."

With that Reynolds had the gray horse brought to the front, and one of the Union privates handed the rope to Peters. Likewise, Ward handed the reins of the horse with Rosen mounted on it to the captain.

With it appearing that the tension had now relaxed and Ward hoped they would be allowed to pass, Reynolds had one more question: "So what's with your man on the sled, there?"

Ward answered, "A rattlesnake spooked his horse, which threw him. We're going to try to find a farmer that'll take care of him until his broke leg heals."

Reynolds nodded his head, and replied, "I'm sure you'll be able to find a place out on the main road that will take him. Then what are your plans?"

Ward lied cleverly, "We're planning to spend a few months helping our friend rebuild his farmhouse that was ransacked. Then we'll split up and head to our homes. We just pray this war may be close to being over."

Reynolds nodded his agreement, "That's what we all hope for, major."

With that, Reynolds ordered his men to separate on the path and make an opening for Ward and his men to pass. Ward noticed that Steinholtz had been writing in a pocket notebook, about the same size as Ward's code book. He assumed that he was making notes of their names, but as he rode by Reynolds, Steinholtz passed Reynolds the folded piece of paper, and Reynolds held it out to Ward and said, "This is a pass that should get you through our lines. Good luck, major." Ward curtly saluted him. Reynolds returned the salute. Ward and his men breathed a collective sigh of relief. As they passed the last two Union soldiers, Captain Reynolds looked after them until they were out of sight, and said to Sergeant Steinholtz, "Sergeant, make a notation in your notebook that we found no one on the cow path, only some horseshoe prints in a mud hole, and that Pvt. Rosen had been lost in the woods."

The sergeant grinned, and answered, "Yessir."

Ward's squad rode on, minus one POW, and trailing a sick, gray horse. The rest of the afternoon passed without incident, much to the men's relief. At about five o'clock they came out on the main road.

# Chapter 6

As Ward and Peters walked their horses carefully out on to the main road, Ward looked up and down the road and ordered, "Thompson and Wells: split up and one go north and one go south for about a mile in either direction and check to see if we are being followed or if there are any Yankees up ahead, and report back. We'll start slowly down the road south."

Peters took charge of the pack horse with the travois attached, and the gray horse trailed behind that. After about a half hour or forty-five minutes of moving slowly down the road, the two privates reported back that there were no Yankees in sight, and no one else even on the road in either direction.

With the squad back together, they moved at a better pace for a few more minutes, when the first farm house came in sight. It was down a short lane to the right. As military experience had taught him, Ward studied his surroundings. Down the lane the farm house sat on the right, with a barn on the left. Some distance behind the barn, the ground seemed to dip down over a slight bank. Ward raised his clinched fist in the air, to signal a "stop and hold." Ward alone turned his horse slowly down the lane. When about two thirds down the lane, the door of the farm house opened, and a white haired man stepped out into the yard. He was thin, but with a ramrod straight, upright, bearing. Ward tipped his hat and addressed the gentleman, "Good afternoon, sir."

The man replied, "How are you boys? My name's Anderson."

Ward replied, "My name's Henry Ward, and we're traveling south….and we have an injured man here. We were hoping we could rest for a while and get him and the horses some fresh water."

Anderson said, "I can tell by your bearing and the weapons of you and your friends up there on the road, that you are military men. I know. I been in two wars and I know how a soldier carries hisself."

Ward gave him the usual story that they were paroled Confederate soldiers, traveling south to visit a friend and to help him rebuild his house.

Anderson and Ward remained still, staring at each other for a few seconds. Anderson blinked rapidly and said "Now ain't that something. I ain't a religious man."

Ward began to think the old man was somewhat affected, and started looking on down the main road, to see how far the next farm might be.

Anderson said, "I ain't read no Bible since I was a kid, when my mother was teaching me how to read by reading the Bible to me from cover to cover. Then she made me read some ever day up until when I left home."

Ward squirmed uncomfortably in his saddle.

Anderson continued, "Now why I told you that is that I had a dream last night and a man in a long white robe said to me out of a cloud 'Thou shalt take in a stranger as if he were your own.' I couldn't figger out what that meant, until right now. You all come down to the house and my wife'll fix us some food. Won't be much but we'll share what we have. By the way, my name's Anderson, Zachariah Anderson. My friends call me "Z.T.""

Ward signaled the men to follow him down to the house. Anderson asked each man to tell him their names. When it got to Peters, Anderson asked if he was "one of them Peters's from up in Giles, Bland, and Tazewell counties of Virginia."He said, "My father was from up in those counties, and his family married into the Peters's up there. We're probably related."

Peters answered, "I'll bet we are too. I have listened to my mother talk about the Andersons. She said some of my dad's people married into those Andersons."

That warm exchange eased the tension in the group.

Anderson told them that it would be wise to take the horses out behind the barn and tie them up, so the neighbors wouldn't be any wiser. He added, "Help your injured friend into the house and we'll fix him a place."

As they half-carried Stephens into the house, Anderson said to the plain, olive-skinned woman in the kitchen, "Lorena, see if you can rustle up something for these men."

She merely grunted and turned back to the stove. Ward noticed the sprigs of herbs hanging in the windows and over the sink, and from the ceiling of the kitchen.

Anderson grinned and turned to Ward and his men and explained, "She is half Cherokee, raised by her grandfather, who was some sort of medicine man. Her name has too many 'eehs and yaw-tays'

40

in it for me to remember, so I call her Lorena. She don't speak much Englitch, but she understands it well enough."

When the travelers took two of the three chairs, and the others on two old barrels, Anderson seated himself on the last chair, and told them his story.

Zachariah "Z.T." Anderson was a strange little man. Born in 1794, he was only twenty when he joined the Army and fought under Gen. Andrew Jackson at the Battle of New Orleans in 1814. Really too old in 1847, he lied about his age, so he could rejoin the Army and fight under old Winfield Scott at the Battle of Cerro Gordo, Mexico, during the Mexican War. In 1850, Anderson had been able to purchase the little farm at an auction on the county courthouse steps, for delinquent taxes. He and his wife had lived on the farm for almost fifteen years, and as he bitterly stated, "had a pretty good farm, until a week ago, when the Yankees came by."

Anderson continued, "They took my only two horses, all the chickens they could find, one pig, and worst of all, my old double-barreled shotgun. Only one barrel worked, but it was the only gun I had. Fortunately, we had a few hours warning by our neighbor that they were coming, and I hid a few chickens, and one other pig down over the hill out of sight." He looked down at the floor for a few seconds, shaking his head. He stood up and said, "A couple of you fellers follow me to the barn, and we'll gather some straw to make your injured man a straw mattress."

Ward said, "Wait a minute, we don't need all that work for just a few hours rest."

Anderson said, "Remember my dream. We will keep him here until he gets back on his feet, and you fellers can pick him up on your way back to your homes, after visiting your friend." He smiled and looked at Ward and Peters, as if he knew there was more to their visit to North Carolina than they had revealed.

Ward, Peters, and Thompson followed Anderson to the barn while Wells saw to watering the horses. While they were at the barn, Anderson showed them down over the back of the hill behind the barn, where his split rail fence marked his property boundary. A large part of the fence had fallen in, or been knocked down. Each man gathered a large arm load of straw and they headed back to the house. While they had been gone, Lorena had put together half an old sheet and half an old tattered blanket, evidently with small splinters of wood to take the place of pins. The men stuffed this cover with all their straw, and Lorena handed them a handful of splinters, without a word. They pinned the mattress together, and helped Stephens from a chair onto the mattress. Stephens grimaced with pain, but he didn't complain. He smiled and breathed a sigh after settling in, showing his obvious approval of his new bed.

After a simple meal of a few beans, potatoes from Anderson's cellar, and a rough biscuit for each man, they sat by the fireplace and relaxed. Over the meal, Peters had mentioned that the gray horse had a limp and they didn't know how bad it was. Lorena said her first words to them, which were: "Me look." When she had left to go to the barn, Anderson said, "She knows a lot of Indian remedies and poultices and stuff like that. She grows some kind of herb behind the house, and she'll wrap it in an old rag, wrap it around the bad leg, and it works like a charm."

Ward cleared his throat, and began with, "Mr. Anderson, we don't expect you to take in Sgt. Stephens and he be a burden to you. We have a few dollars of Confederate money and a few dollars of U.S. money we are giving you simply in exchange for his room and board. We hope you will take it."

Anderson looked at Ward for a few seconds, and blinked four times before saying, "Ordinarily, I would refuse your money and say it was an insult. But this war has taken a toll on everyone, and it has taught me that my asinine pride don't feed us. All we are trying to do is survive until this war is over. What I will do is take your room and board money and go into town tomorrow on the old gray horse. The man at the little general store in town is wanting to take only U.S. money, so I can spend those few dollars with him and get a supply of flour, coffee, and beans. But the next farmer up the road here is an idiot and thinks the Confederacy is going to last forever, and he wants Confederate money, so I will spend those few dollars with him, for some of his potatoes and leather britches beans he has bragged about hiding from the Yankees."

After everyone nodded at this agreement, Lorena returned to the house, and said only: "I fix."

Ward said at the end of that conversation, "Mr. Anderson, the four of us would like to stay over until tomorrow, and work tomorrow on repairing your rail fence. With four of us good strapping young men," they chuckled at that phrase, "I think we can pretty well fix it up, if you have a few more rails or if we can cut one or two trees off the back lot. We would do this strictly as an even trade for your hospitality."

Anderson blinked a few times before replying, "That would be appreciated. I have looked at it several times and could not figure out how I could ever get it fixed."

42

At that, Ward asked Anderson, "Me and these three men will make a bed in the barn, if it's all right with you, sir?"

"You're welcome to it," Anderson replied.

The men said goodnight to Stephens, Anderson and his wife, and retired to the barn, where they spread out their bedrolls.

Wells offered the final comment on the day, "Reckon that's the first real Indian I ever seed up close. Even though I grew up in North Carolina, most of the Cherokees were gone when I growed up. Guess they ain't all bad, after all."

The next day dawned clear and sunny. As the four men washed up in an old horse trough behind the barn, they were actually looking forward to doing some honest work. First they scoured the barn for tools. They were sparse and nearly useless. They found one old axe with a homemade handle and an equally old hammer. Between the four, they had two Bowie knives, and a short shovel picked up along the road the day before, no doubt dropped by a passing Yankee soldier. They would have to make do. They did find three timbers inside the barn that could be used to replace some of the broken pieces of rail fence. They dragged the timbers and took their few tools down over the hill to the first break in the fence. They realized after attempting to fit some of the original rails together that they had no nails or pegs. Wells and Thompson went into the woods and began cutting wedges from a hardwood, while Ward and Peters fitted in the rails. The men felt good for the first time in days. Each man remembered performing similar tasks on his own farm back home. They worked sometimes for close to an hour without talking.

After three good hours of rail repair and remounting, Mr. Anderson walked down and said he was leaving on the gray horse for town and the neighbor's. He said, "I'm going to ride bareback, because if I had a saddle on this horse no one around here has seen, they're going to ask questions. I notice the horse doesn't have any brands or marks, so I can say I found him limping along the road, and it still has the poultice tied on it's leg. I also have to go to my neighbor, Mr. Hewitt, to buy the things from him first, because if I stopped at his place on the way back, with bags of food, he would also get suspicious."

Peters asked how far it was to town, and was told about four miles.

The men went back to work and made good progress until they hit the farthest corner of the fence, where the rails had been fastened to an old stump. The stump had rotted, so they had to build a detour around it, and dig a hole for a new upright post, with the small shovel and old axe, which took some time. But by mid- afternoon they had turned the back corner and started on the portion back up toward the barn.

As the men took a break to wipe some sweat, they saw Mr. Anderson ride the horse into the barn, unload his bags of food, and take them into the house. He came back out and walked down to the four men.

"Looks like you men have done some good work, but I heard some startlin' news. President Abraham Lincoln was assassinated last Friday night, by some crazy stage actor named Booth," Anderson said.

All four were shocked, but Peters found his tongue quicker than the others. He asked, "How, where, and have they caught the guy?"

Anderson answered, "It happened at a theater in Washington, and he was shot in the head. A telegram came through in town for the colonel of the Yankee regiment with this news."

Ward said, "I certainly hope they catch the guy quickly and hope he's not a southerner, or they are liable to want to hang us all!"

Anderson said, "I thought about that on the way home. I will have to keep your man Stephens a secret, or they will certainly come after him."

The four men, with Anderson trying to help a little, finished the fence in another two hours, and sat in the shade of the barn. Ward said, "We need to leave in the morning at first light, and put distance between us and these Yankee regiments up here."

After a delicious dinner that evening, the men sat again by the fireplace, a very quiet group. Anderson asked, "Do any of you have a blank piece of paper?"

Ward looked in the pocket of the saddle bags with the valuable papers in it, and found a piece about half the size of a full sheet of paper. He handed it to Anderson, who said, "Gather around the table and let me draw you a map."

Peters supplied the stub of an old pencil and Anderson showed them that about ten miles south they would hit the old Raleigh & Gaston Railroad tracks that led to Raleigh. No trains had run on it for two years, since one side or the other had burned out three bridges between Raleigh and Richmond. An old wagon road, which had been a supply road when the railroad was being built, ran along side of it for about half the distance to Raleigh. Once it gave out at a rocky cut, they would be on their own again to find a path or trail.

Wells, being from near that area, remarked, "I know that railroad but never noticed the wagon road, but at least I have a general idea of where it goes."

The men thanked Anderson, and they slowly walked back to their beds in the barn, wondering what would await them the next day.

## Chapter 7

A little after dawn, Anderson went out to the barn and invited the four men up to the house for breakfast. He gave them directions on where the road forked, and how they should turn south west to the little crossroads of Ridgeton, which had been a railroad intersection of the Raleigh & Gaston Railroad, and the Roanoke Valley Railroad. He said that at that intersection, just outside of town, they should find the old wagon road. They shook hands and said their goodbyes to Stephens, promising him they would be back for him in a couple of weeks. Anderson walked with the men to their horses, and handed Peters a bag, with some coffee, beans and some cooked potatoes. They thanked Anderson once again for his hospitality and turned their horses south on the road.

←----→

After the initial flurry of activity of the four men packing their horses, talking to Anderson and Stephens, and their heading down the road, things quieted down in the farm house. Mrs. Anderson went outside to work in her herb garden, and Stephens and Mr. Anderson were left alone inside.

Stephens said, "Mr. Anderson, if it wouldn't be too much trouble, could you please cut off the bottom six or seven inches of my brace? If you could, then I could put my foot flat on the floor, and I could start trying to walk. Even if not today, maybe soon."

Anderson replied, "Sure, Elijah, let me find something to cut it with."

He headed out to the barn and soon returned with a short, rusty saw blade, with a rag tied around the handle. He carefully sawed off the bottom overhang of the splint.

Stephens said, "Great, now if you will help me up, let's see if I can hobble to a chair. I am so tired of lying on my back, I would love to just be able to sit upright for awhile."

Anderson said, "First let's take off your belt, holster and gun, and lay them down here on your mattress."

Anderson wrestled Stephens upright without Stephens putting his full weight on the leg with the splint. They made it to the chair, with Stephens carrying a book he had found in his saddle bag. After he was deposited in the chair, with his injured leg outstretched and resting on a small stool, Anderson brought him a drink of cool well water. Stephens looked at the book for the first time. It was a copy of Charles Dickens' *Great Expectations*, part one. It had been given to him by his brother, when he made it home on a furlough over a year ago. He had carried it ever since, meaning to start it sometime. His older brother had been serving in the Giles County Reserves Confederate Regiment at the time. Stephens opened the book and smiled at what was written in the front: "To my brother, Lige, the brave soldier. Keep your head down and your powder dry. Your brother, James."

The next few hours passed quickly, with Stephens the only person in the house. Anderson was out doing something in the barn, and Mrs. Anderson was always working outside in her herbs. Stephens was a slow reader, but enjoyed reading about this little boy nicknamed "Pip."

When Anderson came inside mid-afternoon, Stephens said he was tired and was having some leg pain, so he and Anderson hopped back over to the mattress, and Stephens laid down to rest.

After dinner that evening, Mrs. Anderson went about cleaning up the kitchen. Anderson and Stephens sat and talked. The Anderson's had had a baby in the 50's, a little girl, who had died after a few days, and was buried under a little wooden cross in the back yard. Stephens talked about growing up in Giles County, Virginia, and playing with his brother, James Robert. Anderson recalled his fighting against Santa Anna in Mexico during the Mexican War.

Finally all three were tired, and Anderson blew out the oil lamp and all three went to sleep.

The next day was almost a repeat of the day before, with Stephens spending a few hours in the chair reading *Great Expectations*.

But things were about to change, drastically, for all three.

Just as the Andersons sat down to dinner, with Stephens eating from his plate while propped up on his mattress, there came a knock on the door. The Andersons looked at each other, fearful that it was a Yankee patrol coming back to see what else they could confiscate.

When Anderson answered the door, instead there was only a lone man at the door, wearing a dirty, ragged coat, and an old hat. He said, meekly, "Please sir, I haven't eaten in two days, and could use a crust of bread and a drink of water."

Anderson, being the hospitable man that he was, opened the door and invited him in, showing him to their small kitchen table. Mrs. Anderson filled another plate and put it in front of the stranger, who immediately wolfed it down as if he truly hadn't eaten in days.

After a few minutes of silence, Anderson asked, "Your old coat there looks like a Confederate frock coat. Did you serve in the Confederate Army?"

The straggler wolfed down two more large bites of food and finally answered, "Joined up in August of 1861, and was at the first battle of Bull Run in Virginia with the 10th North Carolina regiment."

"Who was your commanding officer?"

"Col. Ellerbee."

Stephens had been listening closely to this exchange and finally added loudly: "It was called the First Battle of Manassas by us Confederates. It was fought on July 21, 1861. So if you joined in August, you couldn't have been there. And there was no 10th North Carolina regiment at the battle. I know I was there. By the way, Col. Ellerbee was commanding officer of the 8th South Carolina." He ended with, "No soldier ever forgets his commanding officer or gets his unit wrong."

The straggler simply grunted and kept eating. Stephens finished eating and lay back down.

Following the meal, Mrs. Anderson cleared plates and bowls, and Anderson stood up as a signal for the stranger to also stand up and leave. Instead the stranger sat there, looking at Anderson with a strange look on his face. He slowly rose and reached inside his ragged coat, pulling out a large Bowie knife. He smiled an ugly grin, and proclaimed: "Now I think I'll take all your money, the rest of your food, and that gray horse I saw in the barn."

Anderson blinked four times and replied, "We ain't got no money, but we'll be happy to give you a bag of food to take with you, but you can't have my only horse."

The stranger replied, "Do you have a gun?"

Anderson answered, "No, your Yankee buddies took all that and my other two horses."

The stranger then held the large knife up, and smiling, said, "Then I might as well kill you two and your friend over there, and burn the place down. That's what we do to you secesh."

While the stranger was speaking, Anderson casually surveyed the kitchen, looking for a weapon. A large butcher knife would at least make it an equal fight. But Lorena was too neat a cook and housekeeper;

all those weapons were carefully put away. He even looked in by Stephens, hoping to spot his revolver within reach, but it was not visible anywhere.

Anderson looked the man straight in the eye, and said: "I think it's time for you to leave, now."

He replied, "No, not until I slice you three up and clean out the house."

Suddenly, from the straw mattress a few feet away from the three, came Stephens's loud voice, "Judging from your northern accent, and ALL YOUR LIES about fighting at first Manassas, I believe you must be another chicken coward, Yankee deserter. You're a real shit of a coward. Why don't you fight another soldier your own age? Come over here a little closer and I'll kill you just like I've killed a couple dozen damn Yankees."

The stranger bristled, and gritted his teeth. He held out the Bowie knife, and slowly moved toward the man on the mattress. Stephens watched the man carefully, completely covered by an old blanket. When the stranger stopped a few feet away from him, Stephens said, "Now why don't you take that pig-sticker and stick it where the sun don't shine, and get the hell out of this man's house."

With a horrible, bug-eyed growl, the stranger raised the Bowie knife over his head and took another quick step forward. Just as he did, there was a muffled gunshot from under the blanket, and Anderson saw a smoking bullet hole appear in the blanket. The stranger stopped in his tracks, and with a shocked look, looked down at the bullet hole that appeared in his chest. Stephens had fired one shot from his LeMat through the blanket. Nobody spoke a word. The stranger fell slowly to his knees, as if praying to Stephens. As his eyes rolled up in his head, he raised the knife again, and fell forward onto Stephens, plunging the knife into his chest. 1$^{st}$ Sergeant Elijah Stephens, late of the 29$^{th}$ Battalion Virginia Sharpshooters, Confederate States Army, died without saying a word or making a sound. The stranger died at the same instant, and slowly rolled over onto his back, spread eagled onto the floor, his sightless eyes pointing upward toward the ceiling.

For a long minute, not another sound was heard in the house; it was a deathly silence. Finally Anderson realized his wife had had a firm grip on his wrist during the whole incident, and pulled away. Anderson blinked a few times and said, "Well, they're both dead for sure, so they ain't going nowhere, so we'll drag their bodies out back in the morning and bury them. Let's go to bed." Out of respect for Stephens, Anderson walked over and slowly removed the knife from his chest, and closed Lige's eyes.

The couple went to their bed, blew out the oil lamp and laid down, and fell instantly into a peaceful sleep.

Both Andersons awoke the next morning before dawn, and without a word between them, arose and lit the oil lamp and walked into the other room, and looked at the two bodies, which were still exactly in the same positions they had left them. They gently wrapped Stephens's body in the gray blanket, and carried him out the back door, to the tree where their baby was buried. Both of them worked at digging a shallow grave, using the small shovel left by Ward and his men, and the old axe. They placed his body in the grave, gently placing his copy of *Great Expectations* beside him, and gently covered the body with dirt, and patted it down. Anderson found two pieces of wood, from which he fashioned a cross, and tied it together with a leather strip. He found a piece of burnt wood and did his best to write on the cross-piece "Stephens." Next they went back in the house, and dragged out the stranger's body, and without covering it with anything, dug another shallow grave, and rolled the body in, and covered it. Anderson made no effort to make a cross for that grave. He then hung Stephens's belt and holster over his cross, minus the LeMat revolver, which Anderson had kept and put in a kitchen drawer.

They then stood side by side at Stephens's grave and looked down. Anderson removed his hat, and after a few seconds, spoke: "Lord, you ain't heard from me for a long time, but here I am, asking a favor. Please take this good man's spirit to Heaven to be with you. I figure he killed a few people in this damn war, so forgive him for that, because it was a bad war. But he gave his life to save ours, and I've been told that means a lot to you. That's all. So, amen... I guess."

He put on his hat, and started back toward the house, then he stopped, realizing his wife was not with him. He looked back to the grave, and she was rocking on her feet from side to side, and a slow, guttural chant was coming from her lips. Her eyes were closed, and she appeared to be almost in a trance. Anderson had seen this Cherokee death chant only once before, at the death of her grandfather just before they were married. When she stopped, as quickly as she had started, she took one last look and walked to Anderson's side. She took his hand, and Anderson said, almost cheerfully, "Help me hook up our new horse to the plow, I think I'll plow that lower field today."

The reality of their every-day farm life had quickly returned.

50

# Chapter 8

Ward's squad, now down to four men including him, made good time and covered about half the distance from the Anderson farm to the railroad junction of Ridgeton by mid-morning. They had stopped only once, when they came upon a farmer walking in the opposite direction. They asked him what was the latest news regarding the Lincoln assassination, and all he knew was that they had caught and killed "that insane man Booth, and was a lookin' for his helpers." Ward sent Wells and Thompson ahead to scout and check out the little crossroads town of Ridgeton. The two scouts spurred their horses, leaving Ward and Peters behind in the road.

As Wells and Thompson crossed over a small rise a few hours later, they came in view of the town of Ridgeton. Like a lot of small towns, it had been originally named something else. In this case, Ridge Town, but the name was eventually shortened. In some ways it resembled Falls Bluff, with two rows of one and two-story wooden businesses facing a main street, and some dwelling houses at the edge of town. Between the dwelling houses and the downtown business area was a small church and a newly painted one-room school. At the opposite end of Main Street was the stable and blacksmith shop. Jammed together in the middle of town were the doctor's office and the lawyer's office. The most obvious difference in the two towns, was that Ridgeton seemed to have grown up around the small railroad station of the Raleigh & Gaston Railroad, which had come through almost twenty years earlier. Close to the station was a water tank for the steam engines, and a small spur track for railroad car storage. On the spur were two wooden boxcars. The grass was tall around the wheels, and they appeared abandoned. Three small boys were playing in one of the cars, laughing and having a good time. Alongside the spur track was a small railroad maintenance building. As the two slowly rode into town, Wells observed and whispered to Thompson, "This place has a bad feeling about it. Do you feel it?"

As the two men took in the people in view along the streets, Thompson noticed a drunk passed out by the tavern door, and the people

51

standing in front of the store, and the two ladies of ill repute on the balcony of the hotel. He remarked, "They all have stern looks on their faces, and no one is talking. It's like they're all waiting for something...or someone."

Wells replied, "Hope it ain't us."

Thompson said, "It just feels like a bad little town."

As the two riders passed by the tavern, a tall man in a long, black coat stepped out the door and paused to light a short cheroot. He closely watched the two riders, through hooded eyes, out from under a black hat. As he lit his cheroot, his coat hung open, revealing two .44 caliber Colt Army revolvers stuck in his belt. The handles of both pistols were turned outward. His gaze followed the two riders until they were completely past the tavern and had moved on down the street. After a short pause, Mr. Two Colts ducked out his smoke and went back inside. Thompson and Wells continued on at a slow walk until the end of the next block. At that point, Thompson said to Wells, "Looks like our best bet to get some news is at the tavern. Let's turn around and tie up in front."

Thompson and Wells tied up their horses and walked through the door of the tavern into a dimly lit room, with three rough-hewn tables and scattered chairs for customers. A short, bald-headed little man was the bartender. There were two small benches by a square table against the far right wall. A small bar with one rickety stool was on the left of the room. At the back table where three men playing cards. One was Two Colts at the back of the table, with his back to the wall, so he could see the entire room. On his right was Mr. Brown Vest and on his left was Mr. Red Shirt. Thompson recognized the double-breasted, red shirt, as one worn by many of the Confederate soldiers from Texas. They had obviously been playing for hours. Red Shirt slammed down his cards, shoved back his chair and went to the bar for another drink. Brown Vest laughed, and pulled the few dollars of Confederate money toward him. Two Colts stared straight at Thompson and Wells, without saying a word. Brown Vest said, "Howdy, boys, want to set in for a hand or two?"

Thompson nodded and said, "Sure, maybe one or two hands."

Wells moved toward the wall, into the shadows, but where he could watch the table and all the players. Two Colts examined him carefully for a few seconds. He had one of his Colts on the table, by his right hand. Brown Vest had a small derringer by his left hand.

While they waited for Red Shirt to rejoin the game, Thompson asked, "So what's the latest on the Lincoln assassination?"

Brown Vest began to explain, "After Lincoln died on Saturday morning, there was a manhunt like had never been seen. The entire U.S. Army in the Washington area, along with the Pinkertons, and many irate citizens with guns started combing the area around Washington, and even over into Virginia. They finally cornered the killer, this two-bit actor named Booth, in this barn that they set on fire. He either burned up or died in a hail of lead. Ain't nobody clear on that part. They then figured out he had to have had some help, and started questioning everybody where he roomed, and found four accomplices, one of them a woman! Looks like they will all be tried by the Army, and probably all will be shot or hanged, even the woman."

Thompson asked, "So who's president of the U.S., now?"

Brown Vest answered, "It's the vice president, Andrew Johnson. I hear Booth sent somebody to kill him that same Friday night, but I guess the assassin chickened out."

After a pause, he started shuffling the cards. Red Shirt had calmed down, and returned to his seat, and joined the conversation with a shocker for Thompson and Wells: "That ain't the biggest news...the worst part is the Yankees takin' Raleigh and running up the U.S. flag!"

Thompson could not hide his shock and surprise, "What? How did that happen?"

"That coward Gen. Pemberton knew they were coming, but ordered the Confederates to retreat, and the Yankees took over the city. When they found out about Lincoln's assassination, they wanted to burn the city, but fortunately their officers stopped them."

Thompson looked at Wells, who was also shocked, with his mouth hanging open.

Two Colts said his first words since Thompson and Wells had joined the group: "Maybe Pemberton didn't have any choice."

Brown Vest added with a smug look, "You always have a choice of some kind."

Red Shirt added, "Now Governor Lane snuck out of town, and no one knows where he is. So some Union General rode in and says he is in charge of North Carolina's military government."

Thompson and Wells stared at each other for a few quiet seconds, while they tried to absorb all this news.

Thompson finally gained his composure, and casually changed the subject, "Ain't you boys afraid of the law bustin' up this game?"

Two Colts replied, "I been here two days, and found out there ain't no law in Ridgeton. They had a sheriff up until a few days ago, and when he heard the Yankees took Raleigh, he left town during the night. Ain't nobody to replace him."

Brown Vest, obviously running the poker game, said "Ante up, gents, fifty whole cents."

After dealing the hand of five-card, draw poker, Brown Vest won the first hand with three kings. That round went fast and was uneventful. The second hand went almost as quick, with Red Shirt folding and Thompson staying in. Two Colts won that hand which netted him a mediocre $5 pot. The third, fourth and fifth hands went to Brown Vest. After dealing, and everyone staying in and a round of bets and one raise, Brown Vest dealt each player two or three cards. As dealer, he then said, "Dealer takes two."

The two cards had no sooner hit the table, than Brown Vest grabbed them up quickly in his hand. Two Colts, with a snarl, and in one smooth motion, grabbed his Colt, raised it up, cocked it, and had it leveled at Brown Vest's head in a split second. He snarled, "You son of a bitch! That last card came off the bottom!"

Brown Vest didn't try for the derringer, but smiled and said "Now boys, this is just a friendly little game, no use to be a bad loser."

After a tense two second pause of deadly silence, Thompson spoke up, "He's right, I saw it too. I spent months on a Mississippi riverboat, and I seen lots of cheatin'. And you were cheatin'." Thompson quietly looked at the other players, not knowing if either were partners with Brown Vest, and slowly laid his .36 caliber Colt on the table, without taking his eyes off Brown Vest.

After another two seconds of heavy silence, Two Colts said straight to Brown Vest, "Looks like you got maybe one of them choices to make. You stand up slow, don't go for the derringer, and dump the cash out of your pockets you cheated from these gentlemen, and you walk out of here alive. Your other choice ends with your body on the floor with a bullet hole between your eyes…that's your choice."

Brown Vest considered his options, as Two Colts continued to point his revolver at his head, and Thompson's hand rested on his .36 Colt on the table. Without a word of argument, Brown Vest stood up slowly, eased his hands into his pants pockets, and placed two wads of bills on the middle of the table. He looked straight at the players, turned slowly, looked down at his derringer, decided against that move, and turned and walked slowly out the tavern door. The remaining three men each recovered a few bills from the wads, and stuffed them in their pockets. Red Shirt said, "I'm getting the hell outta this town!" and headed for the door. The game was obviously over. The little bartender

54

smiled and chuckled, apparently not concerned at all, and went back to reading a week-old newspaper.

That left Two Colts and Thompson at the table, and Wells walked over to the table, to see what happened next. Two Colts looked toward the bartender, and leaned forward to Thompson, making sure the bartender could not hear him, and extended his hand to Thompson and said in a low voice, "I'm Dan Collins and are either of you Major Ward?"

Thompson, obviously surprised, shook his hand and said also in a low voice, "Neither of us are, but we ride with the Major. I'm Thompson and this is Wells, we were sent ahead to scout this town. He and Lieutenant Peters are a few hours behind us. Now what's going on?"

Dan Collins smiled and said, "I work for Governor Lane, and I know where he is. I'm an agent, courier, or bodyguard, depending on what day it is. I was sent to intercept you before you stumbled into the Yankee hornet's nest at Raleigh."

Collins took another look at the bartender, just as another man entered the tavern. Collins stood up and said, "I don't like the looks of this place, let's head out back."

With Collins in the lead, and Thompson and Wells behind him, the three men went out the back door into the alley.

Thompson revealed what he and Wells had talked about upon entering the town, "We had an uneasy feeling about this town, from the moment we rode in."

Collins said, "I came into town two days ago, and figured from conversations that no squad of strangers had come through, and I figured this was the most likely path you fellows would take. So I gambled that we would cross paths here. Do you have a way of warning the major about this town and where we can meet?"

Thompson replied, "We have a way of posting a coded message on a broadside, and we can let the major know where and when we will meet him."

"Good. Did you two see the railroad maintenance building up by the station?"

"Yes, we saw it. Might be a good place to meet."

"Ok. If the major and the lieutenant show up before dark, let's try to meet them there."

Thompson turned to Wells and said, "Go get one of those papers out of my saddle bags, and that piece of charcoal."

Wells soon returned with the paper and charcoal, and Thompson put it up against the building, and printed an ad for another horse auction. He asked Collins what the next small town was down the tracks.

Thompson finished his coded broadside, with the coded letters "B RR 8," which would translate to "behind the railroad building at 8 pm." He hoped it would be obvious that it was the maintenance building and not the old station, which stood out more in the open.

After the broadside was posted on the hitching post in front of the tavern, Collins suggested, "We have a couple of hours to kill, and my recommendation is that we move to the hotel. At least they have seats and the clientele won't bother us. Also their food is ok, and take my word for it from experience, you don't want to eat at the tavern."

The men moved to the small lobby of the hotel. No one was present at the front desk, so they had the lobby to themselves. Collins and Wells took the horses to the stable down the street, while Thompson waited to pay for one room for the night. After the men came together again, they caught each other up on the happenings of the last week. Collins was surprised that he and Wells may have crossed paths early in the war. Both had enlisted early in 1862, in the 10th North Carolina Battalion of infantry, which was short lived, having never been "perfected" or organized. Wells had been born in Alleghany County when it was part of Ashe County, and Collins had grown up only one county away.

An hour later, the men had a good, hearty, meal in the hotel's small dining room. Surprising for war circumstances, each had a small but well done slice of beef, with potatoes and leatherbritches (dried) beans, and a piece of apple pie, baked that morning.

As they walked back up the street to the tavern for a cigar and a drink, Thompson spotted out of the corner of his eye, Major Ward on his horse heading toward the stable. He and Peters had split up, and Thompson and Ward made no acknowledgement of knowing each other. Ward had to ride by the broadside on the hitching post, and therefore would know about the meeting. Thompson knew they would not see Ward or Peters until the meeting, a procedure the squad had adopted before, when working in a town whose sympathies were questionable.

Collins, Thompson, and Wells enjoyed their cigar and drink at the tavern, and noticed another poker game was going on at the back table. The three men looked at each other, and almost in unison, shook their heads "no," without having to say a word.

Following the drink, the men went back to the hotel and enjoyed the hotel's offer of a .50 cent bath.

As eight o'clock neared and it became dusk, the three men split up, with Thompson and Wells walking on the main street to the railroad buildings, and Collins waiting a few minutes and going over to the back street up by the railroad tracks to the station and maintenance building. They passed Peters, lounging in the shadows of the doorway to the train station, and went back behind the maintenance building. Ward was waiting, and Peters soon joined them. Thompson explained to Ward the happenings of the afternoon and their meeting with Dan Collins, and his news about Governor Lane. Just as they were explaining this to Ward and Peters, Collins rounded the building, and Thompson said quickly, "It's ok, this is Dan Collins, the man sent by Governor Lane."

Collins shook hands with the major and Peters, and proceeded to give them more details about where things stood, "When the governor saw that there was no saving the capitol from the Yankees, he packed up his family and they left in a carriage, headed to his father's house about thirty miles west of Raleigh. He is there now, but we need to move quickly to catch up with him. He talked of sending or taking his family farther away to his father-in-law's house another twenty-five miles southwest."

Ward then showed Collins the hand-drawn map Mr. Anderson had done for them, showing the old wagon road along the railroad tracks of the Raleigh & Gaston Railroad, which eventually led to Raleigh. Collins said, "I figured that would be the route you were headed for, but circumstances have obviously changed. We will still follow the wagon road along the tracks for a few miles, but will cut off before the railroad turns south for Raleigh. I am to escort you and show you the way to cut across country to Coalton, the little town where Lane is staying. Let's leave right at dawn tomorrow morning, ok?"

Ward agreed and the men split up, with Wells happy to sleep in the hay at the stables with the horses; Thompson, Ward, and Peters would sleep in the same room at the hotel, and Collins, with a wry grin, said he had other plans for the night. Thompson remembered seeing the "loose ladies" on the hotel balcony. At least some of the other men would get a good night's sleep.

The Ambush
Original artwork by Jeff Dickinson, illustrator

58

# Chapter 9

Ward and Peters were up and ready to go at dawn. Thompson had to be shaken twice, to get him awake and moving. As they walked to the barn to check on Wells, they encountered Collins stumbling out of the alley beside the hotel. His clothes were only partially on and fastened, and his hair was ruffled. "You look like death warmed over," Ward chuckled.

Collins mumbled, "Why did you let me drink that much?"

Ward replied, "You brought all that on yourself, without any help, my friend."

"Not quite true. I vaguely remember a young lady was helping me."

"You should have slept in the stable with Wells, I think you would smell better than you do now, and probably feel better." All three chuckled at Collins.

After seeing that Wells had the horses packed and ready, the group went back to the hotel for a quick breakfast, highlighted by everyone pouring Collins full of coffee to sober him up.

At last Collins and the squad were mounted and on their way out of Ridgeton. Collins took the lead, and just outside of town the railroad forked, and they found the wagon road beside the Raleigh & Gaston Railroad tracks. Ward took out his compass he kept in the same pocket as the code book. That was the first time any of the squad knew he even had a compass. He carefully checked his directions, and they turned to their left and to the southwest.

For the next few hours the men rode along at a good gait, without much talking. They tried to pry out of Collins just what he had done the night before, but he kept mum, except he had met a girl, and he had a hangover. By afternoon, the terrain changed and the road widened. Judging from the wheel marks, and ruts, it was traveled more often than the road they had been traveling. They began to pass more farms than forest.

After passing medium sized farms with large barns and houses sitting back hundreds of yards from the wagon road, they came to a smaller house, closer to the road. It was neat, clean, and had a large vegetable garden to the left of the house. There was a small barn behind the house. They slowed down, as Collins almost stopped at the lane going down to the house. He pointed out a large, brass lantern on a post by the porch. It was the kind of ship's lantern that had four lenses, one on each side. There was a red lens on one side, a green on another, a yellow on the third, and a clear lens on the fourth. The green lens was turned toward the road. Collins explained that the man who lived there was an old friend, and the green lens was a code signal that everything was safe and there were no threats in the area. Collins stated, "That's our invitation."

The five men turned down the road and stopped near the front porch. Immediately a tall man came out. He was at least six feet tall, with a body like a boxer, or a blacksmith. He had a thick head of black hair. He came out waving at Collins, shouting "Collins, you old son of a bitch, I heard that you were dead, shot by some jealous husband."

Collins jumped down, and they vigorously shook hands and slapped each other on the back. He turned and introduced his friend to Ward and the squad: "Gentlemen, meet my friend, Pete Myers. Pete was a gunner's mate on the Confederate war ships *Sumter* and *Alabama*, two of the greatest fighting ships in the Confederate Navy."

Myers invited all the men inside for a drink. Before going in, Myers advised them to take their horses out back behind the barn to get them out of sight. Once inside, they all stopped just inside the door, and marveled at what they saw. Almost every inch of mantle, shelf, or wall space was occupied by wonderfully detailed wooden sailing ship models. Some were in large bottles, others on wooden mounts, and a few mounted directly on the wall. Most were of three or four-masted sailing ships.

Peters exclaimed, "My gosh, did you make all of these?"

He answered, "Yep, sure did."

Their host found six glasses, not all alike, and poured a healthy shot of whiskey in each, and one for himself. Myers said, "Gentlemen, raise your glasses to Robert E. Lee, the greatest general who ever commanded an army, and to the flag of the dying Confederacy."

Myers saw several strange looks on their faces, about his last words of the salute, he said, "Oh, come on, we all know this whole thing is on its last legs. I felt it when they sank the *Alabama* in Cherbourg Harbor in France last year. A bunch of us dived over the side and got picked up. It ain't even been a year since I dove off the sinking bow of the *Alabama*. And Lee's surrender kinda puts the period at the end of the sentence. As I'm sure you fellows know, Lee got pretty good surrender

60

terms from Grant, and rumor has it that Joseph Johnston is about ready to ask for the same terms so he can surrender."

Ward had mixed emotions when he heard that, because he felt that would truly be the end of the war. Then what would he do? All the more reason for them to ride on and try to complete their mission.

After a good meal prepared by Myers's African-American cook, Cathy, who much to everyone's surprise joined the men at the table, Myers enlightened the others that Cathy was a free person, and was paid a good wage for the work she did.

As darkness approached, and the table had been cleared, Ward, Peters, Collins, and Myers sat down for an after-dinner drink and a cigar, readily supplied by their host. Thompson and Wells watched for a while, then went outside to check on the horses, and unrolled their bedrolls in the barn on some clean straw, and settled down for the night.

The four men sat at the table and relived the war, from the beginning. All agreed that what happened in Virginia and North Carolina was unfair. It was the old problem that the volunteers were promised they were only "for local defense," but when taken into Confederate service, were sent to another state, and did that make it lawful for those men to desert? The discussion eventually got around to the strategic decisions (good and bad) made by inexperienced generals. Peters gave up first, and trudged off to a cot that Myers had showed him in his workshop. So the remaining three discussed the current mission of Ward and the squad. Myers believed that with the recent word he had received, that Governor Lane was still in Coalton, but that Collins and the squad should leave first thing next morning to meet up with him. With a few more drinks, and more dissection of how the Confederacy lost North Carolina and particularly Raleigh to the Yanks, the three were talked out, and wandered off to bed about midnight. Ward and Collins went to their horses, retrieved their bedrolls, and said good night and thanks to their host. They ended up sleeping on the floor in a vacant room upstairs, and fell into a deep sleep.

The men were up early the next morning, and went out to the barn, saddled up their horses, loaded them, and checked cinches. They mounted up and moved out to the lane by the house. Myers came out of the house with a large bag, which he handed Wells, who was the last man in the line. He said, "Cathy didn't want you fellows to leave without a little food to eat along the way. Plenty of biscuits and ham in there. Good luck!" After saying their goodbyes to Myers and thanking him for his hospitality, the squad headed back onto the road.

The group made good time until just before noon, when the tracks took a long curve to their left, and according to Ward's compass, that's where the railroad headed directly south to Raleigh. Collins agreed, and he told the others, "This is where we leave the wagon road, and we head a little southwest instead of following the tracks to Raleigh. If we head right along this tree line, I think we hit another road in a few miles." His memory was indeed correct. After a few miles they found a smaller road that headed in the right direction. It was not much wider than the cowpath they had been on a few days earlier. Almost immediately they were back in the woods, and had to move in single file. After a few miles on the narrow road, Peters became uneasy. He started fidgeting in his saddle, and said in low tone to Ward, "Looks like a great place for an ambush!" No sooner were the words out of his mouth, than things happened.

Something struck the nearest tree, and a piece of bark flew, and Ward grabbed his left arm, with the exclamation "DAMN!" The bullet had missed its target, and ricocheted off the tree, nicking Ward's arm. The shot had come from the woods on their right. A second rifle shot hit the pack horse, bringing it to its knees. Another shot from the woods took off Peters' hat, and probably some hair with it. By that time, the men had all jumped from their horses, and went for cover behind trees, or on the ground. Ward yelled "They'll try to shoot the horses, run them off, we can catch them later." The men took off their hats, yelled war whoops, and waved the hats at the horses, which turned and trotted at a slow pace off down the road. Andy was the last horse to leave the men. One bushwacker stepped from behind a tree and raised his gun, as Collins fired both Colt .44's at the same time, the bullets striking the man in the chest. He fell backwards, with his gun flying out of his hands. Three or four more guns erupted from behind a large fallen log, and the squad returned fire. With both sides pinned down, Ward rolled over and took a serious look at their position. He noticed Collins was on the far left, behind a large tree, and that Peters and Thompson were on the far right, almost in a ravine. He waved to get Peters' attention, and tried to talk without yelling, "Peters, take your globe-sighted rifle and Thompson's Enfield, and see if you can crawl on down that ravine, and come up on their flank." Peters nodded, to show he understand the major's order. He took both rifles, and bent almost double, shuffled quickly on down the ravine.

The major took a moment and used a large bandana and with his right hand and with his teeth he was able to wrap the bandana around his wounded arm, and tied it around the bullet graze. Meanwhile he turned to

62

Wells, who was next to him on his left. Wells had fired one blast from his shotgun, and was trying to reload. Ward noticed an unusual amount of sweat pouring down his face, and saw the young man was shaking, trying to insert his ramrod down the barrel, but missing the whole gun. He grabbed Wells, and shook him until his teeth rattled. He growled at him, "Get hold of yourself. If each of us doesn't shoot at these bushwackers, we may not get out of here alive! You've been shot at before, now SHOOT BACK!"

Wells took a deep breath, nodded "yes" at the major, and got a grip on his gun and was able to reload the weapon.

Ward said to Collins, "How many do you count?"

He replied, "I counted probably five different guns, possibly six, but I think only two are rifles, the rest pistols."

As firing lulled for a moment, Ward noticed one of the bushwackers had a foot and ankle stuck out from behind his log. He nodded at Wells and pointed at the man's foot. Wells grinned, raised his shotgun around the tree, took aim and fired both barrels. The man screamed as he tried to pull his bloody foot back out of sight. He wasn't dead, but he would have a tough time reloading and getting in position to shoot.

At almost the same instant as the man pulling his bloody foot back, there came a rifle shot from their far right, and aimed at the bushwackers. Ward recognized the sound of Peters's globe-sighted rifle. He had indeed flanked the bushwackers. One man went down, probably for good. Before the others realized the source of the flanking shot, Peters had immediately rolled over twice to his right, coming up by a stump, raised Thompson's Enfield, and fired a shot into the other bushwackers, apparently hitting one.

With this element of surprise, Ward and Collins took the opportunity to move forward and to their left, heading for the other flank of the attackers. They stopped and dropped behind two trees closer to the fallen tree that hid the bushwackers. Ward fired the last two shots from his Remington .44, and rolled on his back to reload. The Remington had one big advantage over some other revolvers, in if you had a second loaded six-shot cylinder, you could drop the tamper arm, pull out the pin holding the cylinder in place, discard the spent cylinder, and put a loaded cylinder in its place, insert the pin, and raise the tamper arm, and Ward was ready with another six shots.

Thompson took aim and emptied his five-shot Colt revolver, holding down two of the bushwackers on one end of the fallen log.

Ward counted to himself, what he believed to be the bushwackers' casualties. Collins had definitely killed one, as had Peters' first shot. Wells had wounded the one by a shotgun blast to his foot and ankle. Peters had probably severely wounded another with his second shot. Ward thought he had perhaps winged one. Assuming that Peters was okay and back in the ravine, then their only wounded was himself, that he knew of.

Even though Collins and Ward were in a much closer position, they could not get an open shot at the bushwackers, due to two large trees that were too close together to shoot through the gap. But for the moment, all was quiet. Ward couldn't see Peters, and didn't know if he was still on their flank, or back in the ravine. After another two minutes of silence, Ward yelled out: "Hey, leader of your squad, I believe you are in pretty bad shape. We know of two dead and two wounded. It's up to you how this ends. We can stay here all day, and pick you off, one at a time, or we can rush you from three sides, and kill the rest of you. Or if you lay down your guns and surrender, then I give you my word as a Confederate officer, that no harm will come to you and your men. We are a group of paroled Confederates, just looking to help out an old friend fix up his house, outside of Raleigh. So we just want to move on down the road, probably as much as you do." Then they waited.

Collins whispered, "In about three feet to my left, I can get a clear shot. What do you think?"

Ward replied, "Let's wait for a response from them, either bullets or a surrender."

After another minute, lasting an eternity, slowly a long, three-band musket barrel rose out from behind the fallen log, with a large white handkerchief tied on the end. It slowly waved back and forth a few times.

Ward said, "A smart move. Now you and your men lay down your guns, and stand up slowly, with your hands in the air. There are several guns aimed at you so don't try anything stupid."

Slowly the man who had waved the white flag of surrender rose and made a show of laying down his gun, and raising his hands. Immediately, another stood up, threw down his rifle, and raised his hands. The leader looked down to his left, and said "My other two that are still alive have laid down their weapons. We surrender."

Collins and Ward stepped cautiously out from behind their trees, but with their pistols still leveled at the bushwackers. Ward looked past them, and saw Peters also stand up on their other flank, and walked forward, holding Thompson's Enfield, and with his globe-sighted rifle slung over his shoulder. Last to come forward were Thompson and Wells, still holding their guns at the ready.

Ward ordered, "Thompson and Wells, gather up their guns and pile them over there in the trees. We'll burn them later…and make sure they don't have any others hidden in their pockets."

After all the weapons had been collected and the bushwackers searched, Ward and Collins had them to sit in a tight little group, so they could be watched easier. Ward gave additional orders, "Wells, stand guard with your shotgun. Peters and Thompson take two of their horses and ride down the road and roundup our horses."

The leader of the bushwackers, named Ben, asked for permission to check on his two wounded men. He took an old shirt and wrapped it around the bleeding foot and ankle of the man Wells had shot with the shotgun. When he checked the other man wounded by Peters in his flank attack, he found that that man was already dead. So out of the six attackers, one was wounded and only two were uninjured. Ward said to the prisoners, "You two who didn't get hit take something and bury your three dead friends." The two begrudgingly drug the bodies back in an open spot in the woods, with Collins guarding them closely. One asked permission to get a small shovel from one of the horses, and Ward said, "He can go, I'll watch him." Eventually, the two prisoners dug three shallow graves, rolled their dead comrades into the holes, and piled rocks on top of each. No one said any words over the recently deceased. That took over an hour, and by the time they were finished, Peters and Thompson had returned with the squad's horses that had run off when the shooting had started.

Ward and Collins had a whispered council of war off to one side. Collins asked, "What are we going to do with those three prisoners, just shoot them?"

Ward thought for a moment and replied, "No, I don't want to do that. I promised them they wouldn't be harmed if they surrendered. But it's also too many problems with taking them along, and trying to turn them in to the law. I think we give them three horses, and send them back toward Ridgeton. I think they are scared enough not to try anything."

Ward walked over to Ben and the other forlorn looking prisoners. He said, "Okay, here's the deal I have for you. First of all we don't shoot you, like some of my men think you deserve. We let you take three horses, and you head back north to Ridgeton. There's a doctor there for your friend with the shot up foot. You can tell the doctor in Ridgeton that your injured man had a hunting accident." Two or three on

65

both sides snickered at that one. We will have two of our men hang back and act as a rear guard, so don't try anything." Ward continued, "Do we have a deal?"

Ben replied meekly, "Yes, sir."

Ward asked one last question, "I'm real curious, what was your plan and why did you ambush us?"

Ben responded, looking at the ground: "We had heard that a group of people were coming down this road, to escape from some Yankees, and just hoped to get some easy money and supplies."

Ward said, "Well, it didn't work, now did it?"

Ben didn't say a word, he just looked at the ground and shook his head "no."

Ward checked with his squad, and they had their horses saddled and cinches checked, and they took the packs off the poor pack horse, which had died from that first gunshot. At last they were ready to head out. He went to Ben and said, "Get your wounded man up on one horse, and you and your buddy take two horses and get the hell out of here, heading back to Ridgeton. Got it?"

Ben said, "Yes, sir." He and the other uninjured man helped the wounded man up on one horse, and they mounted two others, and without another word on either side, they turned out onto the main road, and headed back toward Ridgeton.

Ward took the sturdiest looking horse of the ones that had belonged to the dead bushwackers, and loaded it up with their supplies, replacing their dead pack horse. He slapped the rump of the remaining two horses, sending them further into the woods.

Their one last chore was to destroy the guns they had taken from the bushwackers. Thompson found only one pistol that looked to be in reasonable condition, which he stuck in his belt. The other guns were busted against trees and the pieces thrown into the deep woods.

They loaded up their horses, and headed back out on the road, in the opposite direction from Ridgeton.

## Chapter 10

As soon as they got going at a good gait, Collins said, "I think we can make it to Coalton before dark, if we pick up the pace a little bit." Everyone was certainly in favor of that, so they spurred their horses from a walk to a trot. After the shootout of just a few hours before, they all wanted to find a safe haven somewhere. Ward was also anxious to complete his mission.

The group spread out a little, needing more room to move at the fast trot. Ward and Collins were up front, reliving war experiences. Peters was behind them, lost in his own world. Thompson and Wells rode side by side in the rear, taking turns leading the pack horse. After a long period of silence, Wells spoke in a low voice to Thompson, "So what's the story about you and Ward running in to each other on a steamboat before the war?"

"Yeah, I don't talk much about that."

"Come on, I'm not going to tell anyone."

"Okay, you better not. I was deep into a poker game in the smoking room on this boat, but I was pretty plastered. One of the bar girls came by, and this jerk reached for her rear, and made a dirty remark to her. I yelled at him to stop, and he just smirked. I have a quick temper, and I jumped up to slug him, and he whipped out a derringer and aimed it at me. I was too dizzy to try to get my own pistol out of my pocket, and really thought he was going to shoot me.

"What kind of pistol did you have in your pocket?" asked Wells.

"It was an old six-shot Pepperbox I had won in another poker game. Just as this guy cocked his derringer, Ward was off to one side, and too far away to jump him, but he threw an empty whiskey glass and knocked the gun out of his hand. It must have busted the guy's hand. He screamed and ran out of the smoking room. The next thing I remember is waking up in Ward's little stateroom. It was very early in the morning, and Ward was beside the bunk holding a bucket close to me, sitting there asleep, and I had obviously been vomiting all night. I felt so ashamed, I told him I didn't need that bucket…and immediately vomited. It was a long night. When I finally got a little settled, neither of us could sleep, so we talked about things: our families, where we were from, and where we were going. We found out we were much alike in a lot of ways, and became friends. That's why when he wanted me to join this squad, I agreed in a heartbeat."

Wells replied, "Great story, did you quit drinking after that?"

"Nope, Sure didn't."

As the squad neared Coalton, with Collins in the lead, the men noticed a change in the lay of the land. After traveling for two days through wooded areas with some small bottoms along a river, the scenery began to open up to wider bottoms, and wider distances between the hills on opposite sides of a stream. The farms were larger and most were more diversified, in that they were not only crop-growing farms, but also with more cattle and horses visible. The larger farms also began to sport larger houses, not the smaller, plain, clapboard houses in the area where Myers had lived. These houses resembled the Southern plantation style of home: two or three storied, spread out with a large veranda, and most had vertical columns out front. Around most were outbuildings, one being the kitchen, one a small dwelling house for house servants, and sometimes a third for a storage cellar or a separate office of some kind. The houses that were older were shaded by large, centuries old trees, flanking a veranda. The men began to see some houses with the wagon road that circled in front of the house. For the most part, the lawns were well kept and trimmed.

As they rode into the town itself, it also looked different. It had a different feeling about it. While there were several houses to the east of the business section, they were larger, mostly two storied, with large yards, and were very clean in appearance and looked as if newly painted. Just as they entered the business section, Ward noticed something that certainly made Coalton different from Falls Bluff or Ridgeton: telegraph poles that appeared new, with a telegraph wire between them. He wondered if that line was established for the governor, or to connect to a railroad station. The business area displayed the usual offices, general store, church, hotels, taverns, and blacksmith shop. The difference again was the "newly-painted" appearance of almost all the buildings, and the clean streets. The men and women in the streets were nicely dressed, with several of the men wearing top hats, and the women with bright bonnets and small cloth handbags. Unlike the funeral pall over Ridgeton, most of the citizens on the streets seemed to be talking and smiling. It was almost five pm, and some offices were beginning to close. The man at the general store was moving some things inside, preparing to lock the door. Between one small office and the hotel was a small, unimpressive, little building with "Western Union Telegraph Company" painted on the window. Ward wondered how a small,

68

unimportant town like Coalton could rate a telegraph company office. Sure enough, he looked at the telegraph poles on the opposite side of the street, and a wire branched off the main wire, and ran across the street directly to the Western Union office. Also baffling, was that the main telegraph line continued on down the street, and apparently out of town. As they neared the center of town, Collins motioned to Ward to turn his men into a wide alley down by the hotel. Collins tied his horse up in front of the Western Union office and briskly stepped inside. He was only inside for half a minute, while Ward and the squad carefully eyed the streets. No one seemed to notice them.

Collins came out, mounted his horse, and rode up beside of Ward. He said with a big smile, "Good news! The governor's house is wired up to the telegraph line. He has his own telegraph key. We should be able to get some news of what is going on when we get there. I had my friend there in the office telegraph the governor that we are on our way. The governor will have a good dinner ready for us."

With the encouragement of a hot meal ahead, the squad turned and headed briskly out of town. Collins jokingly commented, "I think all we will have to do is follow the telegraph wires." With him in the lead, the men spurred their horses along at a crisp walk. The west end of Coalton was like the east end, with the fields opening up, and a few large well-kept houses on each side. In about ten minutes, they were out of the town and in another half hour, they came to a lane turning off to the right, along with the telegraph wires. Well back from the road, a large plantation-style house appeared at the end of the lane. It had a large wing added on the back, making the house in the form of a large "T." On the wide veranda along the front of the house, were servants setting two large tables, and putting down white tablecloths. With a smile on his face, Collins exclaimed, "We're here!" As they approached the house, they saw an old man with a cane, slowly raise himself from a large porch chair. Coming out the door toward them was a large man, with gray hair and a large, droopy mustache. From a sketch in a newspaper, Ward knew the large man to be Governor Harrison Lane. The men dismounted, as one of the servants came forward to help with the horses. The Governor came forward and shook hands warmly with Collins, and said "Well, I see you found them."

To which Collins replied, "Yes, sir, found them in Ridgeton. We had a little excitement along the way."

The Governor interrupted, "Just hold on to that, we'll have time to swap stories after dinner." He stepped up to Ward, took his hand, and said, "I take you to be Major Ward. Welcome to my home."

"Yes, sir, and we are relieved and happy to have made it."

The Governor walked to the others and introduced himself and shook the hand of each man in the squad. They followed him to the house and stepped up on the veranda, and he showed them where they could hang their weapons. As they turned to enter the house, two women came through the front door, which Peters quickly held open for them. Each was carrying a large plate of food, one of fried chicken, and one of potatoes. After they had placed the platters on the large tables, the Governor said, "Let me introduce my family: this lady is my wife, Rosalee, and the young woman, my daughter, Charlotte, who is seventeen. The little man just inside the door is our son, Robert, who is ten, and his hairy friend is his dog, Malachi. The gentleman with the cane is my father, Abraham Lane." He addressed his father: "These men have come all the way from Richmond to visit us."

The elder Mr. Lane gave a formal nod of his head.

The ladies curtsied briefly, and said "Pleased to meet you, gentlemen."

The Governor then turned to the servants, and introduced them as John, Lucy, and Betsy, and Betsy's husband, Samuel, and he clearly made the point, "These four people are not slaves, but paid workers for us. When they were freed, they chose to stay with us and help with taking care of my father and the children."

Rosalee stepped forward to Ward, and said, "I see your arm is injured, Major, let's go inside and we'll see if we can't clean it up and bandage it properly before we eat."

He replied, "Thank you, ma'am."

Charlotte followed the two down a hallway and into a small room where some of the food was being prepared, after being brought in from the outside kitchen. Charlotte, without being asked, retrieved a basin, poured in fresh water from a pitcher, and brought some clean, white cloth. Rosalee set him in a chair and untied the injured arm, and Ward unbuttoned and pulled off that side of his shirt. Without a word between them, Rosalee cleaned the wound, with Charlotte's help. Ward heard a short gasp from Charlotte, when she saw a large, puncture scar on his upper shoulder, and a large healed gash along his side. Rosalee said, "Well, Major, I see you have seen some action in recent years. Don't worry, Charlotte and I both have worked in the hospital in Raleigh for the last year, and have seen the war at its ugliest." They bandaged the arm with a wrap of clean white cloth.

While the women attended to Ward's injury, the others chatted on the porch, and were shown around the house where they could wash

70

up, while the Governor assisted with carrying the rest of the food to the tables.

When Rosalee, Charlotte, and Ward came back out onto the Veranda, Ward was wearing a new, clean shirt, which must have belonged to the Governor, as it was a little large.

Dinner was a wonderful, friendly, meal with conversations about where each man was from, and a little about each man's family. Seating at the tables seemed to be at random, and unplanned, except that Charlotte seemed to maneuver herself so she was sitting directly across from Will Wells. She looked up shyly and smiled at him.

After the meal and much sharing of happenings during the war, shadows began to lengthen and it grew toward dusk. The Governor invited everyone to move inside. They were shown into a large drawing room, where John offered a small glass of brandy to each adult. Rosalee seated herself at the piano, and proceeded to play "Lorena," and "The Bonnie Blue Flag," and some wonderful pieces of southern music, including one by Stephen Foster. After a time, the elder Mr. Lane and young Robert, both obviously tired, excused themselves and Lucy and Betsy helped them upstairs to get ready for bed. As the remaining group laughed and talked, Charlotte took her mother's place at the piano, and proceeded to softly play some old classic pieces. She was seen to be looking at Wells, as if she was playing only for him. The Governor caught Ward's eye, and motioned for him to follow, and also signaled for Collins to join them. They adjourned to another room across the hall, which appeared to be a temporary office, with papers stacked on and around a large desk. In the middle of the desk was a telegraph key. Ward observed the path of the wire, which ran over to a window and out to the pole by the road.

After the offer of a cigar, and more small talk, the Governor smiled and looked at Ward, and asked: "Well, Major, I believe you have something for me?"

"Yes, sir, it is sent by President Davis. I'll get it from my bags."

"If I'm not mistaken, I believe John has already placed your saddlebags in the hallway."

Ward stepped into the hallway, retrieved his saddlebags and came back into the office. He opened one and took out the large pouch with the papers that had been brought all the way from Richmond. He handed it to the Governor and said, "President Davis expressed his hope that these could help rebuild not just North Carolina but perhaps some of the other southern states. I gathered from his words that he somehow knew that the end of the war was eminent and that the Confederacy would not finish well."

Governor Lane, not surprised by that last sentence, simply nodded and opened the pouch. Everything was quiet in the room for the next several minutes, while Lane carefully went over every paper, absorbing the contents and meaning of each document. He took a few more minutes while he decoded the message from Davis, which he did without comment. Finally, he removed his glasses and said, "Now I see why Davis only entrusted you and your men with this. He must have a tremendous amount of confidence in you and your squad. These bearer bonds hopefully will help restore some of the things that have been destroyed in our state."

"Thank you, Governor. But I am curious. Who can you communicate with on the telegraph?" Ward inquired.

Lane explained that after the railroad station was burned at Raleigh when the Union Army took over, they ran a telegraph wire over into another small railroad building and put a desk in it. He continued, "The U.S. Army runs the telegraph by day, but they leave it unguarded and unmanned at night. I send carefully worded or coded messages to the railroad shack, using the address of: 'RGRRa,' for Raleigh and Gaston Railroad at Raleigh. If our friend is there and listening, he responds by sending 'HCL,' for Governor Lane."

The Governor said, "We need to wait until about eleven o'clock or midnight before trying to send a message, to make sure the Yanks have all gone to bed or to the corner tavern. But there is another piece of business we need to finish before then. Please ask your three men to come in and join us, and John if he is out there."

Ward was at a loss as to what the Governor had in mind, but went out in the hallway and located Peters, Thompson, and Wells, who were standing and talking with the two women and John. He motioned for the four men to come with him in to the office.

Once inside, the Governor asked John to fetch the strongbox stored in the closet. When it was placed in front of him, he opened it and took out a stack of U.S. currency. He said, "Before someone complains, this is not money taken from the North Carolina Treasury, it is some of my personal funds." He counted four stacks, each totaling $250 and passed one stack to Ward and one to each of the men of Ward's squad, and thanked each man for his individual bravery and perseverance in helping to make the journey and deliver the valuable papers. Each man thanked the Governor in awkward replies, as they were caught totally by surprise.

Ward said, more to his men than to Lane, "We can't forget Lige Stephens, who is recuperating at Mr. Anderson's. Let's each man kick in fifty dollars, so we can give him his equal share on our way home."

Lane immediately said, "I won't hear of that. Here is his equal share, which I will entrust to Major Ward." He counted out another $250 and placed it in an envelope, wrote "Stephens" on the outside, and handed it to Ward.

After an awkward moment of silence, when Ward and the others looked at Collins, and wondered why he wasn't receiving pay for his work, the Governor noticed and said, "Dan, I consider what you have been doing as adequate payment of the debt as we both agreed to one year ago. So you are now free and clear and can leave whenever you like. I will write a paper that releases you from the debt forever."

Collins replied, "Thanks, Governor, but I think I'll stick around for a while, if that's ok."

"Good, I can use you at least for the next couple of weeks."

At that point, there was a soft knock at the door, and Rosalee stepped in, and said that beds were ready for everyone, and John would show those who wanted to retire to their rooms. The Governor interjected that Ward, Collins, and he still had more business to discuss and they would stay with him in the office a while longer. Thompson, Peters, and Wells said their thanks again, and wished the remaining three men a good evening, and followed John upstairs.

After they had left, and the door was again shut, the Governor gained a more serious look on his face, and told Collins and Ward, what he was afraid was going to happen next: "I have heard from my contact in Raleigh that the Union Army commander is probably going to send a detail to take me back to Raleigh. Since their argument is that when I left the capitol, that I stopped being the governor, they have put in a Union man as governor. But as you can see, I've been conducting state business right here in this house, just on a limited basis. But there are several complicated and involved actions going on in the capitol, even with me gone, and they probably would either like my counsel, or just to show the people that they are somewhat willing to cooperate with me and some others in running the state."

Ward and Collins both grumbled and shook their heads after that remark.

But Lane ignored them and continued, "I have already asked Mason O'Brien, the state Attorney General, to come by at his earliest convenience tomorrow morning. He was a law partner with me in Asheville before the war, and his family home is only a few miles away.

73

He is completely trustworthy and I want him to take this packet of valuable papers to a small bank he does business with, and deposit them there in its safe. The bank manager is a good friend of mine, and he will guard them with his life." After a pause, he remarked bitterly, "I have got to anticipate the worst case; that a Union Army squad could come here, and search the house, and confiscate or burn my papers and perhaps anything else they feel like destroying."

The other two men admitted that it would be regrettable after all their risk in delivering the papers, to have them burned by the Union Army.

As the three killed time until eleven o'clock, by discussing several other things that had occurred in Raleigh and North Carolina overall, Lane stared at the floor for a moment, and mentioned, as if he was talking to himself, that he wondered what would happen with his warehouse on the north side of Raleigh. He mentioned that it contained supplies, a few pieces of furniture, a trunk of paper files, and two large stacks of blank newsprint paper. He didn't even know if it was still intact or not, but would try to find out from his contact, and figure out what to do. He remarked that maybe he should just have someone burn the building.

Ward was suddenly very interested in that stack of blank newsprint. He leaned forward and said, "I have a perfect use for the blank newsprint, if we had some way of sneaking it out of Raleigh. There's a small weekly newspaper in Falls Bluff, just across the state line in Virginia, which is in desperate need of that paper. The paper is run by a good friend."

Collins grinned, and chimed in with, "I think I have the answer. I have to confess that I have a friend in Raleigh that has a nice buckboard wagon with a false bottom that I have used to transport some things north into Virginia. He is completely trustworthy and has made trips up that way in the past few months, and he knows how to get through the Union lines. He always takes along some extra tobacco or whiskey or something he uses as a bribe. If they come after you, Governor, I want to go back with you, and I will get my man with the wagon on the road to Falls Bluff."

Ward grinned, and took out his envelope of money the Governor had just handed him, and asked what the cost would be.

Collins told him to put away his money, that the man got a cut of things they took north into Virginia, and he would get some pay for this trip, also.

The Governor wisely chose not to ask any more questions about the details.

Finally, the large grandfather clock in the hallway softly struck the hour of eleven. The Governor heard it and remarked, "Let's see if we can raise someone on the telegraph...hopefully a friend!" No one chuckled. The Governor sat at his key, and keyed the address for the Raleigh and Gaston Railroad building in Raleigh. Ward, always interested in codes, watched and listened as the Governor keyed his short inquiry:

··· _ ·_ _ ··_ ···

Ward caught a few letters of the message, but the Governor quickly remarked "That's the word 'status.'" He slowly counted to ten, and sent the same message again. He explained that was one of their signals between himself and the man on the other end, that the Governor would always send a message twice, with ten seconds between, and if a message was ever sent without being repeated, it was someone else messing with their communication. He explained that the one word meant he was seeking the status of things in Raleigh.

The three men sat breathlessly, waiting for a response. In about two minutes, the key began clicking. Lane began writing on his scrap paper. Ward tried to catch a few letters, but his Morse code was a bit shaky. After the clicking of the key stopped, Lane leaned back and showed Ward and Collins what he had received:

SQ7L4U5PM

The Governor grunted and said, "Well, I guess I shouldn't be surprised. The communication is code for: 'Squad of 7 men left for you at 5 pm (today.)' If they left at 5pm, they cannot get here before day after tomorrow. That gives us some time to prepare."

He gave a long sigh, and turned to Ward and said grimly, "Major, I know you thought this mission ended today, and it did. You and your men are hereby released from all responsibilities. You are free to leave at any time. But I am going to ask you to take on one more short mission. I would like for you to escort my family 24 miles southwest to Rosalee's parents' home at Owings Mill. Ordinarily I would ask Collins to do this, but I really need him to go back to Raleigh with me. I could send John, but it would be a problem to send him armed with a weapon, if they got stopped. I am happy to pay some more to each of you and

75

your men that are willing to take on this mission. I just don't want to take a chance on my family being here when the Yankees arrive. "

The major replied, "I won't speak for all my men, without talking to them, but I would be honored to take this last mission. I will bet that the men will agree, but I will ask them in the morning. I don't want any more pay, but I will give the men their say on that offer."

The three men were so intent on the telegraph exchange and what followed, that none of them noticed that the door was slightly ajar. Someone was listening from the third step down from the second floor. Things were about to get interesting upstairs.

Charlotte got up slowly and quietly from the third step, and almost crying, returned to her room, and lit her bedside candle.

Private William Wells was not an ugly young man. Not revealed to the other members of the squad, Wells had had his twentieth birthday a few days earlier, while they were in Falls Bluff. At five foot and ten inches tall, he had a healthy head of dark brown hair, and shining brown eyes. He sported a well-trimmed mustache. He was in very good shape, with a lean body. He was also a light sleeper. There was another bed in his room, which was unoccupied, he assumed it was for Ward or Collins.

When the door to his room opened, with ever the slightest creak, he was instantly awake. His hand came out from under his pillow with his .36 caliber Colt revolver at the ready.

Wells challenged with, "Who goes there?"

The person standing in the doorway was wearing a white night dress, and her long red hair was streaming down on her shoulders. She moved the candle a little closer, and said "It's only me, Charlotte."

Wells fumbled for matches on his nightstand, and lit his candle. He stood up in his long, droopy nightshirt that John had loaned him, from the governor's closet.

"What are you doing in here?"

"I'm lonely and afraid."

"It's not proper for you to be in here."

"But I'm scared. They're talking downstairs about the Yankees coming to take papa, and we're going to be taken to our other grandparents, the Maxwells at Owings Mill. I don't like them."

She took two steps into the room.

"You need to go to your mother's room and let her comfort you."

"But I saw the look in your eyes downstairs at dinner and thought you were attracted to me."

"Charlotte, you are an attractive young woman, but you have to leave."

"Can't I just curl up and sleep next to you? I would keep you nice and warm."

"No, Charlotte you can't. I am betrothed to a young woman in Alleghany County, who has waited through the entire war for me to come home."

"But she doesn't need to know."

"But I will know. And if I confessed to Sarah what we did, maybe she wouldn't forgive me or want me anymore. And what if you meet a wonderful man in a year or two and you feel like you need to tell him about this night? You'll be ashamed, and maybe he wouldn't forgive you or want you. Now I'm not going to risk that for either of us. You need to go to your mother's room, do you understand?

"I guess."

"You're a strong and intelligent young woman, and you'll be just fine."

Reluctantly, she turned and walked slowly out of the room, shutting the door behind her.

Wells placed his Colt back under his pillow, flopped down on it, and stared at the ceiling. Not much sleep for Private Wells that night.

Ward and Collins finally went up to bed about 11:30. The Governor worked on more paperwork until the big clock in the hall struck midnight. He decided to send one more telegraph message. He sat at his telegraph key and keyed, not coded, in plain text:

wheresjohnstons army

He waited the usual ten seconds and resent the message. He stayed up and worked on papers until 1:30 am. He received no reply.

## Chapter 11

The major was up bright and early, knocking on the bedroom door where Peters and Thompson were sleeping. He stuck his head in the door and said, "Downstairs in the Governor's office in fifteen minutes." When he went to deliver the message to Wells he found him already up and getting dressed. He told him the same thing he had told Peters and Thompson.

When the four reconvened in the downstairs office, Ward addressed the men: "The Governor got a late telegraph message, warning him that a squad of Union cavalry has already left Raleigh coming to take him back there. We have no idea if it is as a prisoner or as a friend. Collins is going back with him. Since Lane doesn't know if they are coming to destroy his papers and burn the house, or exactly what, he doesn't want his family to be here when they arrive. He asked me to escort his family to his in-laws house at Owings Mill, about 24 miles to the southwest. I have agreed. I did not commit any of you and you are free to say 'no.' Before you decide, you should know that the Governor has offered to pay some extra money to any of you who will go along. I declined the money, but each of you can decide on your own. But I need to know now who is going and who isn't."

The three looked at each other, nodded their heads and Peters said to Ward, "Looks like we're all going. And tell the Governor that we have benefitted enough from his generosity and we won't accept any additional money."

Ward replied, "Good, I was hoping you would all agree to go."

When the four stepped outside into the hallway, the Governor was coming down the stairs, and said "I need to discuss this with my family. Are you gentlemen through with the office?"

Ward replied, "Yes, sir, and I am happy to say all four of us will be escorting your family. And none of us want any additional money, you have been generous enough."

The Governor must have given his family a wake-up knock also, as the two women and Robert all came down the stairs together. He motioned them into the office and shut the door.

He told his wife, daughter, and son the same thing that Ward had told his men, with some additions: "I want you to pack what clothes and things you might need for weeks. I have no way of knowing when I will be able to send for you. Rosalee, your mother and father have workers at their place to run the mill and help with the house work, so I decided against sending any of the servants from here with you. It's too late to put Robert in school there, and it has probably adjourned for the summer, already. So Robert, take some of your favorite books, so you can do some reading this summer. Charlotte, you do the same. As soon as I can, I will write to you and let you know what is happening. Now let's have breakfast, and then start packing, and tell John and Samuel to hitch up the light carriage for you three, and the small buckboard for your trunks and suitcases. Major Ward and his three men will be escorting you." The Governor thought it odd that Rosalee and Robert were certainly surprised and shocked by the news, but Charlotte was neither.

Their light carriage was a small four-wheeled vehicle, with seating for four people, a top, leaf springs, and light wheels. It had a separate seat up front for the driver. Some variations were called a phaeton or a surrey.

With the two meetings over, the groups went in to the large dining room where Betsy and Lucy had prepared large platters of eggs, ham, grits and biscuits for breakfast. The conversation around the table was subdued, to say the least. The Governor did say that he wanted them to be on the road by noon, but they couldn't make the whole trip that day: "You can stop overnight at the inn at Porter's Crossroads. Major, it's about eleven miles from here, and other than two roads crossing, it's just the inn and a general store and two houses. Rosalee will tell you when you are getting close."

Robert suddenly asked urgently, "I can take Malachi, can't I, poppa?"

Lane smiled and said, "Of course you can."

Robert brightened considerably after that was decided.

Collins came in and mumbled, "Sorry I overslept."

After breakfast, they all scattered in different directions, with the Governor and Collins going into the office, and the women and Robert going upstairs to pack. Ward, Peters, Thompson, and Wells went out behind the house, Samuel brought several buckets of water for them, and they each enjoyed a quick bath in an old bronze tub. John and Samuel then began harnessing the horses and hitching them to the carriage and the buckboard. Samuel introduced the men to the horses, "This here's King George that will be pulling the carriage, and you want him out front. He is a canter, so you just let him set the pace, and he can cover the miles at a good pace. Prince Charlie here will be pulling the buckboard, and he is not a canter, but has a good trot. Just let King George set the pace, and after a mile or so, Charlie will match his pace. They did this coming from Raleigh."

While they were working with the horses, Ward got beside Wells, and asked him quietly, "What went on last night? As I came upstairs, I thought I saw Charlotte with a candle going back to her room, and I could see a light under your door. What happened?"

Wells explained that nothing happened, that Charlotte was just scared because she had overheard about the Yanks coming to take her father, and she was looking for comfort. "I sent her to her mother. That's all."

After about an hour of working with the horses and wagons, and moving them around in front of the house, Ward and the squad saddled and packed their horses. A small black carriage pulled by a large, brown horse, and occupied by one man, pulled into the lane in front of the house. A small man with a valise stepped down and headed for the house. He wore a small, round hat, and had a beak nose like a hawk. He immediately stopped, extended his hand, and said, "Well, Major Ward, we meet again, I'm Mason O'Brien." Ward slowly recalled that the two had indeed met before, at the inn south of Richmond, when Jefferson Davis had met with Ward. The Governor must have heard him arrive, as he came out the door, he motioned for O'Brien, and said "Major Ward, why don't you join us."

Ward and O'Brien went in to the Governor's office, where Collins was already seated. The Governor started by bringing O'Brien up to date on what was happening. He finished by handing O'Brien the packet of bearer bonds, and instructing him to deposit them for safekeeping in their bank's safe. He then handed him another large folder and explained, "These are personal papers of mine, mainly land deeds to this property and other tracts and buildings I own. Please deposit them with the other pouch. I don't know how long it will be before I can pick them up, so I place them in your care. And I want these two men to know where the papers are, and who you are, just in case something happens."

O'Brien said sternly, "Governor, I will leave immediately and have them in the bank's safe before close of their business day."

After O'Brien had left, Ward and the others helped John and Samuel bring downstairs two large trunks and two large suitcases, loaded with clothes and books. They carried them outside and loaded them on the buckboard. The women each also had a hatbox they loaded onto the back of the carriage. The men shook hands with the Governor, wishing him good luck back in Raleigh, and the women and Robert hugged him and had a short, tearful farewell. At last everyone but Robert was loaded in the carriage or mounted. Robert looked for Malachi, who jumped up into the back of the buckboard. Robert told his mother, "I want to ride in the buckboard with Mr. Thompson so I can talk to Malachi." Rosalee agreed without argument. John brought a large burlap sack that clunked and rattled, and put it in the back of the buckboard. He said to Thompson, "Here's some tools you might need, if you have any wagon or wheel problems." He was followed by Lucy, who handed a wicker basket containing some food for the group, covered by a white cloth, to Rosalee who placed it in their carriage.

The small convoy headed out the lane, Peters on his horse was first, spaced fifty feet in front of the carriage. The carriage was driven by Ward, with Rosalee and Charlotte inside. Ward's horse was tied to the back of the carriage. Next came the buckboard, driven by Thompson with Robert beside him, and Malachi watching from behind the seat. Thompson's horse was tied to the back of the buckboard. Wells on his horse brought up the rear, several feet behind the buckboard. As John had instructed, Ward gave King George his head and after about a half mile, he was up to a good canter, without much effort. It took a little longer for Prince Charlie to get up to the same speed, but at last they were all moving at a coordinated pace.

After a short while, Thompson sought to strike up a conversation with Robert. He asked, "Do you know where the name 'Malachi' comes from?"

Robert answered quickly, "Of course, he was the last prophet of the Old Testament, which means he is the last book before the New Testament in our Bible." Thompson was impressed by Robert's intelligent answer. After several more minutes, Thompson noticed him staring at the Colt revolver stuck in his belt. Instead of asking a question, Robert said, "I have a pistol, too, you know."

Thompson looked at the boy and asked, "You are talking about a toy wooden pistol, right?"

"Not a toy at all, it is a single-shot pocket pistol."

"Is it loaded?"

"Of course it is."

"Did your dad show you how to shoot it?"

"Yes, we went out three times and he showed me how to cock it and shoot it at an old stump."

"I hope he taught you that it is not a toy, and you don't point it at anybody unless they are threatening you or your family."

"That's almost his exact words."

Thompson thought all this over for a while, and finally said, "I hope you will never have to use it against someone."

Robert just grinned, and said, "I'll be ready if I have to."

After about four or five miles, Peters signaled from up front to stop. There was a nice, grassy clearing by the creek, and would be perfect to water the horses, and have lunch. After helping Robert and the women down, Ward and Thompson pulled the carriage and the buckboard to the edge of the creek, to let King George and Prince Charlie drink without having to unharness them. While the men unhitched their own horses and led them down to the creek, the women spread a quilt on the grass, and unpacked the food from the basket. It consisted of a block of cheese, some slices of ham from breakfast, a pone of sourdough bread, and several apples. Thompson and Wells simply picked up a slice of each and an apple, and went back to where they could watch the road. Peters picked up his food, and went to watch the horses. Ward sat with the women and Robert while they ate. Rosalee broke the silence by saying, "My parents, the Maxwells, run the Owings Mill. Their house is close by, and they have two servants named Thomas and Mary. On days when they grind corn or wheat, a neighbor, old Mr. Jameson comes over and helps father operate the mill. That's usually on Fridays. It's been a few months since I received a letter from them, but in the last one, father mentioned that the mill needed some work done, but all the able-bodied men were away."

Ward replied, "Mike Thompson's family operates a mill in Wythe County, Virginia. I'll ask him to talk with your father and see what needs fixing."

After the brief stop, they tied the two horses back to the rear of the carriage and buckboard, and everyone loaded back up. After heading back out on the road, King George quickly got up to a good canter, and Prince Charlie matched his pace much sooner than when they had started out in the morning. The road was in fairly good condition, without deep ruts, and they were able to keep up the pace for the remaining miles.

Finally, Rosalee told Ward, "We're getting close to the inn at Porter's Crossroads; I remember this old, abandoned barn on the left." They soon came to the crossroads, and found the inn. It was a typical, two-story, clapboard building with an added wing. Mr. and Mrs. Porter were pleased to meet them all, and they remembered Rosalee and Charlotte. Mr. Porter came out and showed the men where to pull the carriage and buckboard, and they unharnessed King George and Prince Charlie and led them into the small barn. The men's four horses were put inside a large, fenced area behind the barn.

The men came back into the inn, and sat and talked in front of the fireplace in the front room, while Rosalee and Charlotte helped Mrs. Porter and her servant, Jenny, prepare the evening meal. The dinner was plain, but the highlight was the fresh apple pie Mrs. Porter had baked that morning.

By the time the meal was over, and the women had cleaned up and washed all the dishes, it was dark. Mr. Porter said, "The beds are upstairs and have been made up fresh. I only have six beds, so someone may have to sleep down here on the setee. Peters spoke up, "I have a good bedroll, and I'll sleep here on the floor in front of the fireplace."

The night passed without incident. Everyone woke in the morning to the smell of potatoes and homemade sausage frying. After a hearty breakfast, the men harnessed King George and Prince Charlie up to the carriage and buckboard. Ward and Thompson's horses were tied on the back. Everyone said their goodbyes; Ward handed Mr. Porter the money for their room and board, and thanked the Porters for their hospitality, and they turned their caravan back out on the road.

It was immediately obvious that the road beyond the inn toward Owings Mill was not as smooth as what they had been over the day before. There were more rocks in the road, and visible ruts here and there. It was almost impossible for King George to keep up his canter, which slowed the procession down.

About three or four miles from the inn, they came to a rough place in the road, where a tree had fallen across it, but someone had moved it off to the side. It must have laid there for some time, as there was a rut all the way across the road, where it must have been. Fortunately, they were going slow enough, that the carriage, with its narrow wheels and good springs, eased into it, and up and out of it with no problem. But when the buckboard's front wheels eased into the rut and out of it, it jerked a little forward, and when the back wheels went into it, there was a bump, and the rear of the wagon dropped almost down on the road. Thompson yelled, "WHOA! I NEED SOME HELP HERE!" Wells came up from his rear guard position, and he and Thompson were looking at it, when Ward walked back to examine the situation. The good news was that neither the wheel nor the axle appeared to have been broken. But the shock of hitting the rut had knocked the axle cap off, and the wheel had turned partially under the wagon and was jammed. Wells went to the other side, and stuck his head under the wagon and called back, "The axle is ok, it didn't break." The men unloaded the two trunks and two large suitcases, which had shifted toward the left side and to the back of the buckboard. Peters, who said he had worked on some wagons before, and Thompson, went through the bag of tools John had put on the wagon for just this type of situation. Peters took out the small sledge and a large crowbar. He instructed Thompson and Wells to lift the rear of the wagon, so he could knock the wheel back where it was supposed to be. When everyone was in position, Peters said, "On the count of three: …one-two-three." The rear of the wagon came up to level; Ward helped pull the wheel back, and Thompson took his sledge and gave it two licks to get it back in position. That along with some adjustment put the wheel back where it should have been. He found the axle cap, and tried to turn it back on the axle, but the threads had been partially stripped. Peters remembered that in the bag of tools were some metal wedges, probably used to wedge and split logs. One was smaller than the others, only about five inches long, and the men were able to wedge it between the axle cap and the axle, and with a couple of light taps with the sledge, it appeared that the cap would stay in position. They rocked the buckboard a little forward and backward as a test, the wheel seemed to be on straight and solid, and the axle cap stayed in place.

The men loaded the trunks and suitcases back on the buckboard, and they were ready to start out again. This time, Ward had Wells ride just behind the buckboard, so he could watch the rear axle.

Traveling slowly and carefully, the group encountered no more problems on the road, and after a long three hours, they arrived at Owings Mill.

Owings Mill after the repairs.

## Chapter 12

The procession passed several small farms on the outskirts, before reaching the business part of town. The larger farms in the area were on the other side of the mill, west of town. The town of Owings Mill was somewhat larger than most of the other small towns Ward had passed through in Virginia and North Carolina, as it was the county seat or "county town" of Fitche County. The town had grown up just east of the mill and the Maxwell's home. The business area centered around a two-story, brick, county courthouse. It appeared to be the only brick building in town. Facing the courthouse on three sides were small lawyers' offices, the magistrate's office, the sheriff's office, and a surveyor's office. Ward noticed a doctor's office, the usual two-story clapboard hotel, and a tavern. The one church and small school were across the street from the courthouse. The general store and the hardware store sat across from the blacksmith shop. The procession had to pass through all the business area of town to get to the Maxwell's home and the mill, which sat a little back from the road just outside of town. There were small groups of people outside the courthouse talking. Ward guessed it must have been "court day." It reminded him of what Governor Lane had said, that he was most proud of his accomplishment that, unlike all the other southern states, he had not suspended the rule of *habeas corpus*, and had worked to keep the courts fully operational during the war. People stopped talking and watched as the procession passed through town, and two people in front of the general store recognized the Lane's carriage, and waved at Rosalee and Charlotte. Rosalee recognized one, and said "Hello, Mr. Jameson." A small boy, about Robert's age, ran beside the buckboard, and yelled "Hi, Bobby!" Robert returned the shout, and said "Good to see you, Jimmy." Some of the men on the street sternly eyed all the weapons of the four men in the convoy.

As the procession reached the outskirts of town, Rosalee pointed out the mill and house up a lane to the right of the road. Ward could see the painted words, now faint, on the side of the mill which read "Owings Mill." As they neared the house, the door opened and a tall, well-built, grey-haired man stepped out on the porch, followed by a shorter woman, both with big smiles on their faces. A servant came around the house to help with the horses and the carriage. Rosalee didn't wait to be helped down from the carriage, but held up her skirts and jumped down as her father walked quickly to welcome her with a firm hug. Charlotte waited to be helped down by Ward. As soon as the buckboard came to a halt, Robert and Malachi jumped down and ran toward the man, shouting a greeting of "Grandpa Max!" Mr. Maxwell said to Rosalee, "Welcome home, daughter." When he welcomed Charlotte, she said in an icy tone: "Hello, grandfather." There was a minute or two that followed, of earnest and quick words from Rosalee to her father. He wrinkled his forehead and concentrated seriously on every word. Ward knew that she was explaining what had happened with the governor, and the reason for their unannounced visit. Maxwell then looked toward Ward, stepped forward with his hand extended and said "I'm Reuben Maxwell and this is my wife, Clara. Thank you for escorting the family here safely, welcome to our home." Robert and Malachi were talking happily to Mrs. Maxwell as introductions were made of the men of Ward's squad. Maxwell's two servants were introduced as Thomas and Mary. Thomas showed Wells and Thompson where to pull the carriage and buckboard, and they unharnessed the horses. They led the horses through a gate into a large field where they could be free to graze. Under Maxwell's direction, Peters and Ward unloaded the trunks and suitcases from the buckboard and carried them inside. After the unloading Maxwell said to the two men to wait in his library, "I want to hear more details about what is going on with the governor." He pointed them to a room off the downstairs hallway.

The two men were amazed by what they saw in the room. It was covered wall to wall and floor to ceiling with bookshelves. Ward walked around the large library and marveled at the many rows of books. Maxwell had indeed built a collection that would be the envy of any state library. Ward noticed such titles as John Marshall's two volumes on the life of George Washington, Bancroft's 1852 *History of the United States*, William B. Fowle's book on *Familiar Dialogues and Popular Discussions,* books on Greek grammar, farming, and Greek to English dictionaries, French literature, mythology and grammar, books on ancient Greece and Rome, Plutarch's *Lives*, the *Master's Chess Playing Companion*, and Stratton's *Chess Player*, Falconer's Poetry, and works of Coleridge, Whitman, Shelley, Keats, and Byron, and the speeches of Henry Clay. More familiar to him were the works by Milton, and some math books that he had studied in school. He also saw a shelf of the *Revised Statues of Virginia*, and books with sample legal forms. On other shelves were periodicals, such as copies of *Blackwood's Magazine*, the

*Democratic Review*, and the *Edinburgh Review*.He pulled out a copy of S. Augustus Mitchell's *Ancient Geography*, and marveled at the wonderful maps. A voice behind him said, "That's Robert's favorite book." Mr. Maxwell had quietly entered the room and explained, "I went to college to be a teacher, and began collecting all the books I could afford. I really wanted to be a college teacher, but it didn't work out. When Clara's parents, Mr. and Mrs. Owings, died before the war, they left the mill and the house to us, and since then I've spent all my time running the mill and tutoring. I had always thought that occupation would be temporary. But when the war became serious and close to home in 1862, things got tight, and we couldn't have sold the property even if we had wanted to." The two men continued a relaxed conversation about Maxwell's library and the age of some of the books.

Meanwhile, Peters had found a comfortable chair by the window and was completely engrossed in Stratton's book on chess.

While the men were relaxing, Rosalee and Charlotte helped Mary and Clara in the kitchen prepare the evening meal and set the places at the large dining room table. Robert played outside with Malachi, by throwing him a stick to retrieve.

When the meal was prepared and carried to the table, Rosalee told Ward to summons his other three men to come in for dinner. It was crowded with everyone seated around the one table. With Ward's squad of four, Mr. and Mrs. Maxwell, Rosaslee, Robert and Charlotte, it made nine people squeezed in at the table. Mr. Maxwell asked everyone to bow their heads, and he said the well-known grace poem of "Give us, Lord, our daily bread." The atmosphere at the table was warm and friendly, with multiple conversations going at once. Clara, having worked as a nurse for a short period, was especially interested in Rosalee and Charlotte's work at the Raleigh hospital. Mr. Maxwell was interested in hearing the account of Ward's squad and their interesting encounters in getting from Richmond to Coalton and then to Owings Mill. Robert finished first and asked to be excused and went into the library to look at his favorite book. With everyone finished, instead of the men going into the library, Ward asked Maxwell, "Since it is still daylight, could we have a look at the mill. Rosalee said on our trip here that there were some problems that need fixing, and Mike Thompson has worked in his family's mill before the war, and he would like to look at your mill and see if we can be of any help." Maxwell was immediately agreeable, and led the men out to the mill.

Thompson asked, "Did you only grind corn or some wheat?"

Maxwell thought for a few seconds and answered that it had been mostly corn, and remarked that there hadn't been a good wheat crop for several years.

As the men walked around the outside of the mill, Thompson remarked to Maxwell: "This is a well-built mill. It's built on two separate foundations, to prevent the vibrations of the mill machinery from shaking the building apart! Is it about thirty years old?"

Maxwell confirmed that the mill had indeed been built in the 1830's, and added: "It certainly did shake when the mill was grinding at full speed." But the mill was stopped and the water wheel had been stationary for almost a year. The sluice that normally fed the water onto the wheel was diverting the water back into the stream.

The flume or sluice to the mill is a wooden trough for passage of water to the water wheel that drives the mill. It has a small gate for stopping or shunting the water off the wheel. A large gear-wheel called the "pit wheel" is mounted on the same axle as the water wheel and this drives a smaller gear-wheel, the "wallower," which turns the great spur wheel, on a main driveshaft running vertically from the bottom to the top of the building. In this type of mill the great spur wheel was known as the face wheel, and it turned a smaller wheel known as the lantern gear. The lantern gear, often called the cage gear, has round rods for spokes, parallel to the axle and arranged in a circle around it, much like a round bird cage. This system of gearing makes the main shaft turns faster than the water wheel, which rotates at about ten revolutions per minute. The millstones turn at about 100 revolutions per minute, and are laid one on top of the other. The bottom stone, called the "bed," is fixed to the floor, while the top stone, the "runner," is mounted on a separate spindle, driven by the main shaft. The distance between the stones can be varied to produce the grade of flour required; moving the stones closer together produces finer flour. The grain is lifted in sacks onto the "sack floor" at the top of the mill on the hoist. The sacks are emptied into a bin, where the grain falls down through a hopper to the millstones on the floor below. It flows into a hole in the center of the runner stone. The milled grain (flour or meal) is collected from the outer rim of the stones as it emerges through the grooves in the runner stone, and is fed into sacks on the floor. This same process is used for grains such as wheat to make flour, and for maize to make corn meal. The Owings Mill had been an important fixture of the town and the county prior to the war.

Maxwell pointed out the first problem: the fact that two of the slats were broken in the water wheel. Maxwell said, "This problem shouldn't be too hard to fix, as there are some old slats in the mill that are probably spares left when the mill was built. It's just that it takes two or three men to manage the wheel and get the new slats inserted in the slots."

As the group moved into the mill, Maxwell said sternly, "Now here's the bigger problem." He pointed at the cog mechanism that converted the turning water wheel into turning the grinding wheels, and said "See that wooden gear wheel that is on the shaft to the wallower wheel? It is busted, so even if the water wheel was turning, it couldn't convert that power to turn the grinding wheels."

With that, Thompson stepped down onto a small step below the level of the floor, so he could have a closer look. After a minute, he said: "It certainly is busted. It's called the face gear. And so is the lantern gear. Four of its round pegs are broken. The problem is not only making a new gear and repairing the lantern gear, but the shaft will have to be raised enough to remount them."

As the men looked at the gearing and thought about the problem, Thompson looked further down in the pit and exclaimed, "Here's the culprit that caused it!" He stood up, with a short, rusty pry bar in his hand.

Maxwell said, "Now it all makes sense. I have been missing that old tool ever since the mill quit working. Both things seemed to happen around the time Mr. Jameson brought his rowdy grandson over and let him play up in the top of the mill, against my firm orders. That kid has thrown or dropped that pry bar down into the gears!"

Thompson looked at Ward and smiled and nodded his head, and Ward said, "We'd be happy to work on it tomorrow, if you have room to put us up."

Maxwell happily replied, "Gentlemen, you have room and board and our hospitality for as long as you wish to stay."

Peters and Wells, who had been in the back of the group, looked at each other and shrugged their shoulders.

As the group stood and remained silent, while Thompson tried to come up with another method of repair, Maxwell happily exclaimed, "I think I might know the solution. Jacob Schottlemeier, our town blacksmith, used to be a cabinet and chair maker. When we first moved here, he showed me an interesting lathe he has, which is powered by a foot pedal. I think we could ask him to make a new gear. Maybe he will be bored with pounding horseshoes and plow blades, and need a break to do something different. In the morning, if you four gentlemen could raise the shaft, I will slide the old cog off and take it and the lantern gear to show Jacob." Thompson nodded his head in agreement with the plan.

As they stepped out of the mill, Maxwell thought for a moment and said, "With Rosalee, Charlotte, and Robert, our bedrooms in the house are full. But behind the house is a small building that had been used for storage, but when a North Carolina company of infantry camped here for a week in late 1861, they cleaned it out and used it for a bunkhouse. There are four rough bed frames in there and you fellows are welcome to fix your bedrolls and blankets in there however it suits you."

Peters quickly responded with, "I'm sure we'll be just fine there, Mr. Maxwell."

Following a look at the bunkhouse, the four men went to the barn where they had left saddles, bedrolls and blankets, and carried them to the bunkhouse. They spread out their belongings, and sat outside till darkness fell, listening to the strains of Rosalee or Charlotte playing tunes on the Maxwell's piano. Ward stuffed some tobacco in his pipe, lit it and thought of other things. They finally turned in for a much needed rest.

## Chapter 13

The next morning dawned sunny and warm for the end of April. Fog hung low over the stream running along the road into town. After all the men were up and dressed, Maxwell came out to the bunkhouse and invited them down to the house for breakfast. The main topic of conversation was how they were going to repair the mill. Thompson said it would take two or three men in the top floor of the mill, to raise the main vertical axle to where he could get down in the pit and remove the two broken gears off the shaft and axle. He said, "If I can't pull the face gear off the bottom of the shaft, I'll have to knock it off with the little sledge we brought on Governor Lane's buckboard." It was decided that after that Thompson would go into town with Mr. Maxwell, to see the blacksmith about repairing the two gears. Ward, Peters, and Wells would stay at the mill and repair the broken slats in the water wheel.

Ward asked Maxwell if he had any other tools they might use. Maxwell replied, "Yes, there's a small saw, hammer, and a few other things in the rear of the house." Maxwell added as an afterthought, "Thomas, why don't you go ahead and harness Prince Charlie to the buckboard, and ride into town with us. While we are at the blacksmith's, you can go to the general store and see if we can pick up some flour, coffee, bacon, and maybe some beans." Ward and the other three men gathered up the tools and they all headed for the mill.

Once at the mill, Thompson stepped down in the pit where the gears were, and waited for the others to go upstairs to the top of the mill. He soon heard a shout from Peters of: "Ready down below?"

Thompson answered, "Ready."

The task turned out to be not quite as hard as they had expected. The three men upstairs grabbed the vertical axle, and after two shakes from side to side to loosen it, they gave a heave, and the axle rose up almost to the rafters. Thompson yelled, "Just hold it there for a second and let me knock off the two damaged gears." With one hit from the sledge, which knocked the face gear off, and a softer tap to knock the lantern gear off the other axle the two gears were detached. After that was accomplished, the men on the top floor eased the vertical axle back down to its normal position.

Maxwell took Ward to the top floor of the mill, and showed him where the spare slats of wood were laying. Ward confirmed that he and Peters could cut the planks to the right size to replace the damaged slats in the water wheel.

With that, Maxwell and Thompson climbed on the buckboard, and Thomas climbed into the back, and they headed for town. Prince Charlie seemed in an agreeable mood and enjoyed the little jaunt.

They stopped the buckboard in front of the general store, hoping that Thomas could get them at least some meager amount of supplies, while Maxwell and Thompson took the damaged gears and walked across the street to the blacksmith shop. Jacob Schottlemeier was a robust, middle-aged man, with a short red beard. He appeared to be pounding out a bent plow share on his anvil. He stopped, and revealed a wide, tooth-filled grin, as he wiped his hands on his leather apron, and extended his right hand to Maxwell. "Reuben, it's good to see you again." The two men shook hands firmly and were obviously good friends. Maxwell introduced Mike Thompson as a "friend of the governors who is staying at our home for a few days." Thompson and Maxwell proceeded to show Jacob the two damaged gears and described what needed to be done.

Jacob remarked, "The whole town has been wondering what stopped the mill. I think I can help." Under his breath he muttered to Maxwell, "I need a break from pounding horseshoes and plows, anyway." He led them to the back of the shop where some woodworking tools were along the back wall. Thompson commented on having used most of the tools at home. Jacob said, "I think I have a nice piece of hickory to make good spindles for the lantern gear, and I should have a good, solid, piece of either oak or yellow poplar for the face gear. I can turn the spindles on my foot-pedal lathe with no problem. I don't have a large enough piece to replace the entire face gear, but I can make a wedge piece with the four new teeth cut into it, and cut out a hole in your gear, and pound our new piece into the hole." Maxwell and Thompson were both relieved that Jacob could fix the two gears. Jacob turned to Thompson and said, "Looks like you know your way around a tool shop. I could use an extra pair of hands if you're willin'." Thompson happily agreed to help. Maxwell stated he would cross the street to see if Thomas had found anything at the general store, and see if they had a newspaper.

Back at the Maxwell home, while Ward, Peters, and Wells worked on the water wheel, which was on the opposite side of the mill from the house, the women were working inside the house. Robert's friend, Billy, had come over, and the two were playing with Malachi in the far corner of the yard. Malachi anxiously awaited each time for the boys to throw the stick to be fetched again. In the late morning something happened. A strange man walked down the lane and, without hesitating, walked up on the front porch holding what appeared to be an old sack. He wore an old and dirty, long gray coat, down to his ankles and was partially bald on top. He did not see the boys playing because they were out of his sight up in the corner of the yard behind him. Robert stopped. The front door was standing open to let in fresh air, and the man walked straight into the house without knocking. Robert watched this but didn't know what to do. He looked toward the mill, but saw no one. He recalled his father's stern words, "You'll know when its time to do something and you'll know what to do." Robert turned to Billy and said, "You'll have to go home, I have a bad feeling something's going to happen." (Days later, Robert could not recall saying that.) Billy ran for home. Robert hesitated an instant, trying to decide if he should run and get the men at the mill, or go to the house. The silent voice inside him told him to go quickly to the house. He ran to the porch, stepped quietly and tiptoed into the hallway, where he flattened himself against the wall beside the door to the dining room, and listened. The intruder was throwing all the silver pieces from the dining room cupboard into his sack. He had a large .58 caliber horse pistol he was holding on the three women, who were backed against the dining room wall. Robert then knew what to do. Hanging beside him on a peg was the jacket he had worn when he arrived there. He felt in the pocket and retrieved the object he wanted, and slipped it into his baggy pants pocket. He walked timidly into the dining room, and stood with Clara, Roselee and Charlotte against the wall, looking scared and shy. He held his mother's hand and watched the man. To cram the silver into the sack, he had to use two hands, with one holding the sack open. He laid his horse pistol on the dining room table. It was obvious he had told the women he would shoot them if they moved or screamed. When he turned around from loading his sack from the cupboard, he said "Well, I see we have another person in the room. Just stay put little man, and you won't get shot." He pointed at Rosalee, "You, lady, I next want that nice necklace you're wearing." Rosalee gasped and placed her hand on the emerald necklace that Harrison had given her for their anniversary. Forgetting he had left his pistol on the table, he took a step toward

95

Rosalee, and was reaching for her necklace. In an instant, Robert reached in his pants pocket, pulled out his single-shot pistol, cocked it and without hesitating fired a shot into the intruder's right knee. The man was shocked, let out a yell of pain, grabbed his knee and fell to the floor. Charlotte let out a piercing scream and grabbed her head. The wounded man yelled, "DAMN YOU! YOU LITTLE BASTARD, YOU SHOT ME!!" Robert took two steps to the table, grabbed the horse pistol and pointed it at the intruder's head. Everyone froze for a second or two. Then rushing through the door was Peters, followed by Wells, and Ward three steps behind. They had all heard Charlotte's scream. Peters immediately assessed the situation, and carefully reached around Robert and took the horse pistol from his hand, placing his thumb between the cocked hammer and the percussion nipple, so it could not go off. He put the pistol on half-cock and pointed it at the floor. Shaking, Rosalee said, "He was stealing our silver and wanted my necklace, but Robert shot him." Ward patted Robert's shoulder and said, "You did the right thing to protect your family, young man."

Ward turned to Wells and said, "Take one of the horses right now, ride into town and get the sheriff or the magistrate, and the doctor if he's there. Tell Maxwell and Thompson at the blacksmith shop what's happened and to get home." Rosalee and Charlotte regained their composure and Rosalee said, "Charlotte, get the white cloth we keep for bandages, and scissors. Clara, can you can get a pan of water?" Clara, who appeared to be in shock, nodded "yes." With Wells on his way to town, Rosalee and Charlotte proceeded to cut the man's pants leg, wash the wound, and tie a tight bandage around the knee.

With Ward and Peters standing guard, Robert sat down in a dining room chair, as if his legs were suddenly weak. Rosalee and Charlotte finished bandaging the intruder, with Clara assisting. About that time, Mary came in from a trip to the barn. She had missed the entire incident. She saw the old sack still lying on the floor with the silver pieces spilling out of it, and without a word, she began very carefully, almost reverently, placing the silver trays, bowls, and tea set items back in the large dining room cupboard. In less than fifteen minutes, there were hurried footsteps on the front porch. First through the door was Maxwell, who reached out for Clara and Rosalee and took them in his arms. Next inside was a man who turned out to be Magistrate Johnson, and behind him with the familiar black bag was the town doctor. Wells and Thompson brought up the rear. Evidently Wells had explained to the magistrate the circumstances, as he grinned and said, "Well, if it isn't Mr. Taggert. We have met before. I arrested you a year ago but couldn't get a witness to testify or you would be in prison. But good news! You're wanted in Gaston County for robbing and beating that old couple over there, so I'll be sending you to Gaston."

Taggert whined, "But the little bastard shot me!"

Johnson laughed and said, "That's right, you got just what you deserved. Consider yourself lucky the lad didn't kill you!" He proceeded to handcuff the intruder, with the declaration, "With the sheriff out of town, I have the authority to arrest criminals so you are under arrest."

While Johnson had been talking to Taggert, the doctor carefully removed the bandage on his knee, and with one quick flick of his forceps, he yanked out the .36 caliber ball that had been lodged beside part of his kneecap. Taggert screamed out a loud "OUCH!" The doctor ignored the scream, and replaced the bandage.

The magistrate turned to Ward and the others and said, "Two of you men get him under the arms and load him in my carriage. We'll let him recuperate in our luxurious jail cell for a few days while I notify Gaston County to come get the scum."

After the doctor, Magistrate Johnson, and the prisoner left for town, everyone sat down and let the days' events sink in. After a while, Maxwell said, "I need to take the buckboard back to town and pick up Thomas and the supplies, and check with Jacob and see if he was able to fix our two gears for the mill."

Ward stated, "I'd like to ride along, if that's all right."

The two mounted the buckboard and headed down the lane to the road. Maxwell exclaimed, "I can't believe Robert had a little pistol and shot this robber! Where did he get that little gun?"

Ward answered, "His father gave it to him and evidently taught him how to shoot it. And the governor taught Robert not to use it except under very serious circumstances, such as today's situation."

"I'm proud of my grandson for that! Most people would have lost their heads or frozen and not been able to do anything. I think Robert took a large step today toward becoming a young man."

"I agree," Ward said.

They stopped in front of the general store, where Thomas was waiting with half a bag of flour, and smaller bags of beans, coffee, a slab of bacon, and a few ears of corn from last year. He exclaimed, "The whole town is talking about how young Robert shot a robber! Is it true?"

Maxwell took about a minute to explain the happenings, and that all the family was safe and uninjured.

After loading the supplies onto the buckboard, they walked across the street to the blacksmith shop, where Jacob was waiting for them. After Maxwell introduced Major Ward as the leader of the squad that had escorted his daughter and grandchildren from Coalton, Jacob said, "Some excitement at your house, glad everybody's unhurt. I was able to fix the two gears as best as I could. I think they will hold."

Before Maxwell could say anything in response, Ward thanked Jacob and asked what the cost would be for all that work.

Jacob said simply, "I know most folks don't have any money, so just grind me a poke of corn meal when the mill gets working."

Ward reached in his pocket and pulled out a few dollars, and handed Jacob $7.00 in U.S. dollars, and said, "Here's a few dollars to help out."

Maxwell started to object, but Ward stopped him with "You have fed me and my squad and given us a room, this is the least I can do."

Jacob's wide, toothy smile appeared and he said, "Thanks. A few dollars really does help."

Everyone was satisfied. Ward, Maxwell and Thomas headed back to the house with the repaired gears.

Meanwhile, Thompson took Robert into the library and they sat down. Thompson started to say something to Robert to comfort him, but Robert spoke first: "I heard my father's voice inside my head saying I would know when it was time to do something and what to do, and that's why I came straight to the house and didn't try to run and fetch Ward and the others from the mill."

Thompson said in a calming voice, "And you did the right thing. You defended your family and helped stop the criminal without killing him. You are a brave young man and your father will be very proud of you when he hears what happened here today."

Robert smiled and seemed to perk up.

It was between three and four o'clock when Maxwell, Ward, and Thomas returned from town with the supplies and the two repaired gears for the mill. Peters and Wells had finished replacing the slats in the water wheel and were satisfied that it would turn. Thompson and Maxwell prepared to reinsert the two gears on the axles. Once again, Ward, Peters and Wells went to the upper floor of the mill and pulled the vertical axle up far enough for the two men below to slide the face gear onto it. Then they slid the lantern gear on the other axle. After that major step, it took more work to get the two gears anchored onto the axles with lock screws. Dinner was ready about six, and the men were exhausted, but content that they had repaired the mill. Everyone agreed to wait until the first thing in the morning to divert the water back onto the water wheel, and try to grind something.

About seven thirty, as it was getting dusk, a lone rider came down the lane toward the house. Ward, Peters and Wells were sitting on the front porch. Ward looked around, and Peters and Wells were alert and watching closely, with their hands on their weapons. The three men stood up and watched as the rider approached. Ward said, "It's ok, it's John, the governor's servant." John dismounted from his horse which was lathered up and had obviously been pushed hard all day. Maxwell and the others came out on the porch to get the news from John. He stepped up on the porch and said, "The Yankees came for the governor just a little past dawn this morning. They waited while he wrote two letters. One for you, Mrs. Lane, and one for you, Major Ward. They let him ride his own horse, and they didn't handcuff or shackle him. I was afraid old Mr. Abraham Lane might raise a fuss, but he watched them take the governor and ride off without saying a word. Mr. Collins went with them." John handed the letters to Rosalee and Major Ward. Charlotte stood close by Rosalee and read the letter with her:

*My Dearest Rosy,*

*By the time John delivers this message to you, I will be well on my way back to Raleigh to face an uncertain fate. It appears the war is over. I sent Major Ward a letter telling him of Gen. Johnston's surrender and his declaring the war over. So let us hope and pray that it is truly over. I will try to write to you as often as I can from Raleigh, whether I am a prisoner or the new king. I will think of you and the children every day, and will miss you all dearly. Remember how much I love you and I will work to bring us back together as a family with every ounce of strength I have. Take care of yourself and the children. I will always remain,*

*Your loving husband,*
*Harrison*

Rosalee bit her lip and a single tear ran down her cheek. Charlotte simply looked down at the ground. She looked up quickly at Wells, who looked away. Only after they had read their letter, did Ward read his letter:

*Major Ward:*

*By the time John delivers this message to you, I will be well on my way back to Raleigh to face an uncertain fate. Late last night and early this morning I received two telegraph messages from my friend. Gen. Joseph E. Johnston surrendered his Army of Tennessee and the other smaller armies under his command to Union Gen. Sherman yesterday at Durham Station, N.C. He received the same lenient terms that Lee received from Grant. Part of the surrender agreement was the declaration by Johnston that the war was over. With Lee's surrender, Johnston became the ranking general officer in the CS Army, and it is accepted that he had the authority to sign such an agreement. His men are now being paroled. I knew you and your men would need this information immediately. I sincerely wish you and your men a new life and good fortune. John is also delivering a letter to my wife.*

*Your servant, sir,*
*H. C. Lane*

Ward was speechless. Without saying a word, he passed the letter to Peters, who read it and in turn passed it to Thompson and Wells. No one spoke a word for several minutes. Robert, who had not read his father's letter asked, "Is it from daddy? What does he say?"

Robert's mother stated simply, "Your father says he loves us very much and will write for us to come home to him before long." That seemed to satisfy Robert, who went back inside.

Ward and his men looked at each other, but none spoke. It was obvious that each was trying to absorb the realization that the war was finally over.

Governor Lane's servant, John, stayed overnight in the bunkhouse with Ward and his men. They talked until late in the night about the war ending and what it meant. For the area around Owings Mill, it meant that many of the paroled soldiers would be returning home. Other families would be in mourning when their soldier did not return. John finally went to his bunk, turned his face to the wall and fell into a deep sleep.

After a few minutes, Thompson shook his head and said in a low voice, "If only we had one more regiment at Gettysburg, we could have held the high ground at Cemetery Ridge, and maybe…"

Ward cut him off by saying, "There ain't no point in the 'what if's' and 'if onlys,' it's all over and we're done with war!"

Peters turned to Ward and asked, "Do you think Johnston should have kept on fighting?"

"The newspaper Maxwell picked up today quoted Johnston as saying it would have 'been a crime against humanity to continue the war.' Sherman had almost 90,000 men in his front…I guess he did the right thing."

Thompson asked, "Wonder if Stephens has got the news that the war's over?"

Peters replied, "Yeah! What if we're the ones to give him the news?"

All three smiled and chuckled, visualizing the look on their fellow squad member's face, when they would give him the news.

Somewhere in the woods a lone bird chirped his sad song.

## Chapter 14

When Confederate Gen. Joseph E. Johnston surrendered the Army of Tennessee, it totaled approximately 18,700 men, who were paroled. He also surrendered the other armies in his department, including those in Georgia, South Carolina, North Carolina, and Florida. That brought the total of soldiers surrendered to over 89,000. But under Item 2 of the surrender agreement, he agreed to disband all Confederate States armies then in existence, and they were to deposit all their arms. It was the largest single surrender of the Civil War. With his surrender, there were no Confederate armies left east of the Mississippi River. All that was left west of the river were Gen. Kirby Smith's Army of the Trans-Mississippi, and a small brigade of mounted Indians under Gen. Stand Watie.

At breakfast the next morning the main topic was the implications of the war being over. Four years of fear, angst, sorrow and dread were apparently over. It was obvious to Ward and others that Maxwell was anxious to get to the mill and test their repairs, but he remained politely quiet and let the war conversation proceed at its own pace. Wells was oddly quiet and stared at his plate.

Robert, not completely understanding all the adult conversation, asked "Does it mean daddy will be coming home and we can move back to Raleigh?" That stopped the conversation immediately, as his family tried to come up with an answer that would not worry him. Finally Rosalee explained, "They may need your father to help them out in Raleigh and other places for a time, and we will have to wait until we hear from him. Meanwhile I want you to do some reading, young man. And I am sure your friend, Billy, will want to know you are all right after yesterday's incident."

Robert smiled a broad smile and remarked, "You're right! May I be excused? I'd like to go to Billy's if it's all right."

Robert was allowed to go and he grabbed his jacket and headed out the door for the short walk to Billy's, which was between the Maxwell's and the main part of town.

The conversation wound down, with Ward and his men still somewhat in shock. Maxwell looked at Ward without speaking, and Ward knew it was time to go work on the mill. Maxwell, along with Ward and his squad walked out the door and over to the mill in silence. Before getting to the mill, Maxwell asked Ward "If it's not in confidence, could you tell me if there were any more details in your letter from Governor Lane?" Ward explained what Lane had said about Johnston's surrender at Durham Station, and about him signing a declaration that the war was over, and that he surrendered the other armies in the South. Maxwell ended the conversation with the comment, "Thank God! Sounds like the end of the war to me."

When they reached the mill, Thompson checked inside to make sure the main vertical axle was disconnected from the other gears that moved the grinding wheel. After verifying that, Maxwell threw the wooden lever that diverted the water in the sluice onto the water wheel. The men stared for a minute as the water flowed onto the water wheel with no effect. The wheel remained stationary. Peters stepped down into the trough beside the wheel, reached up as far as he could reach on the slats of the wheel, and gave a mighty tug that started the wheel turning. After a minute, it slowed down somewhat, but did continue turning. After another minute or two it apparently had settled to its normal rate of speed, and continued turning on its own. The men were relieved and Maxwell smiled to see this critical part of the mill operating again. They then moved inside where they could see the vertical axle was turning properly. After a pause, Maxwell pushed the lever which moved the vertical axle with the face gear against the lantern gear. For a second there was only a groan as the gears attempted to mesh. Thompson quickly jumped down into the small area beside the gears and gave the axle with the lantern gear a sharp hit with the hammer. With another groan, the gears began turning. With this major bottleneck resolved, they all turned their eyes to the grinding wheel. It began turning slowly, and gradually picked up speed. As the wheel turned faster, the mill began to vibrate. Maxwell yelled "WE DID IT! IT'S WORKING!"

As the men shook hands and Maxwell congratulated them, the last obvious test was to grind something into meal or flour. The day before, Thomas had carried out to the mill half a bag of corn to be ground as a test. Maxwell and Ward began pouring the corn into the large, square, funnel that fed onto the grinding wheel. Wells and

Thompson positioned a large sack where the finished product began coming out from between the two grinding wheels. Maxwell came down to the ground floor, inspected it closely by running it through his fingers, and with great satisfaction declared it to be perfect corn meal.

As the men stood around laughing and talking, Thomas came out from the house to the mill. Maxwell called him over and said, "Thomas, great news! The mill is working. Take one of the horses and ride over to Mr. Jameson's and let him know we are back in business, and for him to pass the word that whenever anyone in the neighborhood has anything to be ground, to bring it over. And tell him I would sincerely appreciate his help again in working the mill, if he's so inclined."

The men made short work of most of the remaining corn they had to grind, and disengaged the gears from turning the grinding wheel, but allowed the water wheel to continue turning. Maxwell scooped a couple of handfuls of the corn meal into an old beat-up metal cup, and happily walked quickly to the house to show the rest of the family the output of the operating mill. Ward headed out of the mill toward the bunkhouse. Wells walked rapidly up beside him, and tapped his arm, and said, "Major, I need to talk to you about something important."

"I think I know what it's probably about."

"I've been trying to figure out what to do. If the war's really over, can I be discharged and head for home?"

"I don't see any reason why not. As far as I'm concerned, our missions and the war are over for us."

"I think my home in Alleghany County is only about thirty or forty miles from here, and that's the closest I have been to home in two years. I hope I still have my fiancé waiting for me."

"Before you leave, let's go in the bunkhouse and I'll give you the copy of your parole. I don't know if you will need it when you get home, but better to be prepared. It worked with that Yank captain back on the cowpath, so I think it would work again if you needed it."

They went in the bunkhouse, and Ward pulled the large leather wallet from his saddlebag, shuffled through it, and finally handed Wells his parole.

Ward looked him straight in the eyes and said, "William Wells, it has been an honor to serve with you, and I wish you nothing but the best of luck and a great future. Soldier, you are dismissed." He extended his hand to Wells.

Wells stiffened to ramrod straight, saluted the major, and then shook his hand. He said, "The honor is mine, major."

The major casually saluted in return, without snapping to attention.

When they left the bunkhouse, John was saddling his horse and preparing to return to the Lane home at Coalton. The three shook hands, and John mounted up and rode down the lane.

Wells rolled up his bedroll, gathered his belongings, and led his horse out of the fence where he saddled him, and continued beside the major toward the mill to say his goodbyes. He shook hands with Peters and Thompson, who wished him much luck and good fortune. As he mounted his horse and turned toward the lane, he looked back at the house, and a lone figure was standing on the porch, watching him. It was Charlotte Lane. Wells tipped his hat to her, and she gave him a small wave, with a white lace handkerchief in her hand. He headed his horse down the lane, turned west on the road, and was soon out of sight.

A little later Thomas and the women came out to the mill and Maxwell re-engaged the grinding gears of the mill and showed them how it was working. The women had brought a small glass of brandy for each of the men. Everyone was elated and they had a small celebration. After much laughing and talking, the group finally separated with Thomas and the women going back to the house.

Ward, Thompson and Peters stepped outside the mill, and Ward said, "We need to talk about what we are going to do. Let's go to the bunkhouse." The three walked in silence to the bunkhouse. Once inside, Ward began the discussion with, "I told Wells I could see no reason why he couldn't go home. I have thought about it a lot since last night, and it doesn't make sense for us to attempt to ride west across the Mississippi and try to join up with Kirby Smith. As soon as hears about Lee's and Johnston's surrenders and the declaration of the end of the war, he'll surrender too."

Peters added, "My thoughts exactly. I guess we could split up and go our own ways, but I want to go back by way of the Andersons and see if Stephens is healed enough to ride."

Thompson added, "And so do I."

Ward concluded with, "I have been thinking the same thing. We need to meet Stephens and give him his share of the governor's money, and hopefully he can ride with you guys up into western Virginia. As for myself, I'm going to go on to Falls Bluff and see how Delia is doing."

Peters and Thompson both grinned and said, "We were wondering if that wouldn't be a stop on your way home to Bedford County."

Ward laughed along with the two, and he suggested, "Since we wouldn't get very far today before dark, what do you say we wait and stay here tonight and leave first thing in the morning?"

The others nodded in agreement. They left the bunkhouse, and headed to the main house, where they found Robert looking at another geography book in Maxwell's library. Peters found his favorite chess book, and Thompson picked some other books at random. They spent a leisurely couple of hours, without thinking about war. Ward asked Maxwell for a small sheet of paper and a pencil and sat and wrote a letter to his mother:

My dear mother,

I'm sorry I haven't written sooner, but we have been so frequently on the move that I haven't had the opportunity. I wanted to let you know that I am doing fine, and my health is good. Myself, Thompson and Peters are at Owings Mill, in western N.C., where we have been helping out some nice people who were having some trouble. I will tell you the whole story when I get home. It appears the war is finally over, and all the Confederate armies in the south have been surrendered and paroled, so we can start home. It will take several days, because we have to go by and fetch Lige Stephens, who was injured by a fall from his horse and has been cared for by a nice couple on a farm above Ridgeton. Wells has already left here headed for his home in Alleghany County, N.C. We will start from here tomorrow morning. Please give my love to Noah, Jonathan, Rachel, and Matthew, and take care of yourself. I Hope to be home soon, and am always

Your loving son,
Henry

Noah was Ward's much younger brother, being only sixteen when the war started, and had stayed at home; Rachel was Ward's sister, and Matthew Grimes was Rachel's husband. Rachel and Matthew had moved in with his mother when Henry had gone off to war. His other brother, Jonathan, who had been twenty-one when the war started, had been conscripted (drafted) by the Confederate Army in 1862, but the family had paid for a substitute, so he had joined the Bedford Home Guards and had thus been able to remain at home.

Ward handed the letter to Maxwell, and asked him if he would post it for him. Maxwell took it and stated, "I hope the mail is working again. It has been off and on for the last two years. The next time the stage comes through, I will make sure it gets on it."

Ward explained to Maxwell that he, Peters, and Thompson would be leaving in the morning and heading for home. Maxwell showed no surprise and said he totally understood.

The three men retired to a last restful night in the bunkhouse. Thompson was sketching something on a sheet of paper. As they each turned in, their talk turned to what they each would do when they reached home. Thompson's idea was the most interesting. He said, "What I was drawing was a sketch of the gears in the Owings Mill. I am convinced I can apply what I learned while repairing the mill to redesign the gears in my family's mill, and make it operate more efficiently."

Peters looked off into space and said, "I imagine I will go back to helping run my father's large farm. He only had two slaves, both of whom have left, so I am sure he is short-handed. I'm looking forward to the peaceful life again."

Ward was strangely silent on the topic. He simply added, "I don't know what I'll do. I need to get home and see my mother and brothers and sister."

## Chapter 15

The next morning the group sat down to another wonderful breakfast with the Maxwells, some realizing it would be the last time they would see each other. Conversation was once again rather subdued. Ward mentioned that they would be going back the way they had come, to pick up Lige Stephens and stop at Falls Bluff. Following the meal, Maxwell asked the three men to step into the library, where he pulled from a drawer a small pocket-size book with a large fold-out map of North Carolina and the bordering part of Virginia. He pointed out a better route. A few miles back to the east they would find a wagon road that followed alongside the Dan River, which flowed to the northeast into Virginia. In places it paralleled the Richmond & Danville Railroad. He showed them where that road intersected the old road heading north to the railroad junction at Ridgeton and then on to Falls Bluff. Ward made a few notes of towns and river crossings in his notebook. Following that discussion, Ward, Peters, and Thompson headed to the bunkhouse where they collected their bedrolls and belongings, and carried them out to the fence where their horses were waiting. They saddled up, loaded their belongings on the pack horse, and led the horses down by the house. Maxwell and the family came out on the porch and the men said their goodbyes. Maxwell again thanked them very earnestly for what they had done for him in repairing the mill, which would benefit not only the Maxwell family, but the whole community. As they said their goodbyes to the ladies, Robert remained unusually quiet.

As the men were about ready to mount up, Robert rushed forward, grabbed Thompson's hand, and said "Thanks for being my friend."

Thompson was temporarily stunned, but shook his hand and said, "It was my pleasure, young man."

Clara handed Ward a sack and explained it contained some bacon, beans, cold fried chicken from the night before, and cornbread for their trip. Ward threw it over the back of the pack horse, and with a final wave, the three men turned their horses down the lane, headed east, and were soon out of sight.

After an uneventful morning, as they distanced themselves from Owings Mill, they began to notice a change along the road. By afternoon they came across discarded items beside the road: broken army canteens, old knapsacks, empty gun belts, even some tattered pieces of uniforms- all grey. Ward concluded that it must have been the leavings thrown aside by some of the paroled soldiers from Johnston's Army finally on their way home.

The first walking soldiers they encountered were from the Confederate infantry, and were heading in the opposite direction. They wore a hodge-podge of tattered uniforms. Some had their buttons all cut off. Some simply trudged past, without looking up. If one stopped and looked at the three mounted men, Ward or the other two would offer him a drink from their canteens. One who stopped and accepted a drink said "Thanks" to Peters, who asked "Where are you coming from, sergeant?"

The man answered, "We were from Johnston's infantry. Before we could leave Durham Station, where we were paroled, some of the Yanks cut off our uniform buttons, because they had the North Carolina symbol on them." A single tear came down his cheek. He added, "That ain't no way to treat a fellow soldier. We weren't his prisoners. We deserve better." With that, he turned and continued at a brisk walk up the road.

The three men rode along, mainly in stunned silence. It was hard to absorb the end of the war and the end of the Confederacy. In another mile or two they encountered three walking tattered soldiers, one of whom limped on a makeshift crutch. Ward and the other two mounted men stopped and offered the men a drink of water from their canteens. All three wore the remnants of Confederate infantry uniforms. The man on the crutch asked, "How much farther to Bryson's Crossroads?"

Ward remembered a small store and inn about an hour's ride from Owings Mill. He answered, "About three or four hours."

The limping man smiled, and said, "Almost home! Let's get going." He picked up his crutch and set out at a crisp speed, while his two friends hurried to catch up.

These strange and sometimes emotional scenes repeated themselves a few more times, until early evening when the shadows began to lengthen. Ward's men found a small clearing off to the side of the road only a few yards from the stream. They let the horses drink, while Peters and Thompson foraged about for dead limbs and sticks for a campfire.

After the campfire was going, the three unsaddled the horses and placed their bedrolls around the campfire, which they had enclosed with rocks. Thompson retrieved their little pot from their utensils that had been on the pack horse. He and Peters did their usual task of putting a few cups of water in the pot, followed by handfuls of their beans, while Ward took his knife and shaved off a few lumps of bacon, and their "bean delight" was soon cooking. Peters placed the larger pieces of their corn bread on three of the flatter rocks around the fire. The three were ready to eat when from the road came a shout: "Hello, the camp!"

From instinct, all three men reached for their guns. Ward stood up and shouted back, "Come in a little closer so we can see you."

Two men stepped forward carefully and slowly. As they came nearer into the light of the campfire, Ward could make out the two unarmed men, in the short gray jackets of Confederate soldiers. The taller soldier in front had the red facing on his jacket sleeves of an artillery officer. The second man had similar trim on his jacket. Ward spotted the two yellow bars on the first man's collar, and said "Welcome, Lieutenant, come join us."

The man stepped forward and said, "I'm Lieutenant Evans and this is Sergeant Bowen. We were paroled a couple of days ago by Gen. Johnston at Durham Station, and we're on our way home."

Ward introduced himself, Peters and Thompson as paroled soldiers from Lee's Army, and previously of the 35th Virginia Infantry.

The Lieutenant remarked he and Bowen just wanted to warm themselves by the campfire if that was ok. He said they had been walking for two days, without much food. Ward invited them to share in their "bean delight," and Peters threw two more handfuls of beans into the simmering pot over the fire.

While the beans were cooking, Ward asked the two men what unit they were in.

Evans replied, "The 4th Battalion, North Carolina Light Artillery."

"I think you men were at Gettysburg, were you not?"

"Yes, we were on the right hand side of the cannon row on the third day."

"We were there, also, and I never seen anything like it."

"It's a shame we didn't win that battle."

After a few moments of silence, Ward asked what happened after Gettysburg, and how they had ended up back in North Carolina.

Evans replied, "We started out in 1863 with four Napoleons and we captured a Whitworth after Gettysburg. That was when we were at maximum strength. But we lost two of the guns in Virginia in February, when one of the iron Napoleons exploded, and another was captured. They reorganized the armies and attached us to Johnston's Army after that. When we surrendered we only had about forty men left in the battalion."

The Napoleons were 12-pounders which were the most common field pieces in the Confederate artillery, although some 10-pounders were made. (The 10 or 12 pounds refers to the weight of the projectile.) They were named after Napoleon III of France. These cannon were cast from brass, then bronze, and finally from iron, as the war progressed, and were smoothbore. The Napoleon was also the most common field piece found in the Union artillery batteries. These cannon could launch solid shot, explosive shells, grapeshot or cannister. The Whitworth was a British-made rifled piece, and was fairly scarce on both sides of the conflict. The Confederacy smuggled theirs in through the blockade. The ones obtained by the Confederacy were probably muzzleloaders, although some breechloaders were made. They could easily fire accurately at 1800 yards. They were either 3 or 6-pounders.

Peters chimed in with, "I'll bet you and the sergeant are glad to be heading home."

The sergeant answered with, "If we still have a home to return to."

All the others nodded their heads and were also worried whether they would have homes to return to.

The lieutenant asked Ward what their story was, and how they had ended up so far west in North Carolina. Ward gave him the usual story of being paroled at Appomattox, and traveling into North Carolina to help a sick friend who needed help with his house.

After the men enjoyed their dinner, Peters fetched an old blanket from the supplies carried on the pack horse, and said "Sorry we don't have anything but this old blanket. But if you two can share it, we'll keep the fire going all night. You're welcome to stay."

The lieutenant replied, "We thank you, sir, for your hospitality."

Ward sat and poked the fire and, as usual, his mind was a hundred miles away.

After a restful night, Ward awoke between 5:30 and 6 am, when the dawn was just breaking. The two artillerymen were already gone, with the old blanket folded neatly where they had slept.

The three men broke camp, saddled the horses, loaded the pack horse, and headed northeast toward the Virginia-North Carolina border. When they came to a fork in the road, they followed Maxwell's directions, and headed to the right which according to Ward's compass took them toward their homes in Virginia.

The men noticed that on this narrower road there were none of the paroled, homeward-bound, ex-Confederate soldiers.

The trio rode for a few hours along the Dan River which flowed northeast into Virginia. The river was running high and fast due to heavy rains in the mountains. The water was beginning to overrun its banks. Peters remarked that the river was definitely in flood stage. Thompson remarked about all the logs and trees riding high on the current. After some time watching the river as they rode along, Ward suddenly held up his fist, meaning "stop and hold." Peters reached for his gun, asking, "What is it, what's up?"

Ward said, "Listen! Do you hear a bell?"

As Thompson and Peters listened, it became louder. There wasn't a school or church anywhere near and the ringing was rapid and almost frantic. They watched behind them, back up river, as the ringing became louder. A small steamboat came into view, and it was in trouble. It was listing and appeared to have lost its steering. Thompson remarked, "Looks like it hit a snag back upriver. It's definitely listing." Both Ward and Thompson had seen snags in the Mississippi when they had traveled by steamboat before the war. As the boat neared, the men made out the name on the side: the "Governor Lane." It was a small, sidewheel batwing boat.

The batwing was designed and built to run on the tributaries of the main rivers in Virginia and Kentucky originally, and was a lightweight, maneuverable, cheap to operate boat. Its paddle wheel was on the side, and they were hardly ever more than a hundred feet long and ranged from twenty feet to twenty-two feet in width. Most of them had one deck and one boiler. They had an uncovered paddle wheel which gave their class its name. These boats generally drafted a foot or less, and weighed less than 100 tons. Their advantage was the shallow draft that allowed them to go up small rivers when the larger packet steamboats were docked due to low water. By the end of the Civil War these ugly little steamboats were running on many of the rivers in the upper South.

As the boat neared, Ward and the others could make out people in the small wheelhouse and on the rail waving frantically. Three were obviously women passengers, and there appeared to be two male passengers. One could be heard yelling frantically, "HELP US! HELP US!"

Ward immediately had an idea. He ordered, "Downriver, fast, a couple of hundred yards. Find the largest overhanging tree. Take a rope and run up the tree to where it will be nearly over the boat when it comes by. Anchor the rope to the tree and throw it down to the man on the front of the boat. Maybe we can pull them into shore."

The final words weren't even out of his mouth before Thompson and Peters were spurring their horses further downriver. Ward gave his horse two slaps of his reigns and the three were riding at top speed. In a few hundred yards, they found a large, overhanging tree and it appeared that its top would reach out far enough to be over the boat when it passed under, assuming the boat stayed in near the bank and not out in the main current.

Ward asked, "Who has the longest rope?"

Peters answered, "I think I have one long enough." He grabbed his rope, stood up in his saddle and jumped onto the tree trunk. He shinnied up the main trunk, and out over the river in seconds. He made one turn of the rope around the trunk and tied it securely with a bowline knot. As he positioned himself and made ready to throw the rope, the ship's mate was up in the front of the listing boat, and realized immediately what the plan was. Peters threw the rope just as the front of the boat passed under the tree. The mate reached out and grabbed the rope, and without wasting any time, passed it through a large iron ring mounted on the deck frame of the boat. He made one loop through the ring, then laid down on his back with his feet against the ring and pulled the rope with all his strength. Fortunately, the tree only bent slightly. The boat was pulled in almost under the tree, and ground against the tree and into the bank. The pilot house of the boat groaned as it jammed against the tree. Miraculously, the boat stopped, jammed against the tree and the bank. The pilot stuck his head out the pilot house door and yelled, "Get the women off first!"

Peters responded, "Hand the first one out."

The women were obviously scared to try this escape down a tree in all their petticoats, but the pilot didn't give them an option. He said to one, "You first, and be quick about it." He grabbed her by the waist and almost threw her out the small door into Peters' waiting arms. A few feet below Peters on the tree was Thompson, waiting. And near the bottom of the tree was Ward also waiting to put the woman on firm ground. The woman reached out and Peters grabbed both her hands, and almost swung her around and down to Thompson who grabbed her, and helped her down the tree trunk into Ward's waiting arms, who swung her to safety on the riverbank.

While this tense episode had been unfolding, a man and a boy rode up in a buckboard to where the horses were, and yelled, "We can help. We live just up the road. We heard the bell clanging and knew it was a boat in trouble. We came as fast as we could."

Immediately the pilot pushed the second woman through the small door and she reached out for Peters' outstretched hands. He passed her down to Thompson. The pilot had the third woman already outside and reaching for Peters. The small boy in the buckboard said, "Look, Poppa, it looks like a bunch of big chickens up in the tree!" With the three women safely on the ground and being helped by the man and his son into the buckboard, the two male passengers were able to climb out onto the tree and make it safely down to the ground. The pilot yelled down to the deck hand, "You go next, Charlie." While Charlie was climbing up the ladder to the pilot house deck, the pilot yelled "I have to go get the engineer from the hold." As he went quickly down the ladder the boat let out another loud groan, and it shifted over at more of an angle. The pilot and engineer came rushing up the back stairway from the lower cabin where water was almost knee deep; the boat was sinking. Just as the engineer came out on the lower deck, the boat took another shift further over on her side. The engineer was almost thrown overboard and half-jumped and half-fell into the water beside the boat. Unfortunately it was deeper than he thought and he went under. After a few seconds, Ward started to throw off his jacket and gun belt to jump in the water after him. Thompson yelled, "Don't jump in, major; look at the water. It's making a whirlpool, and that's what pulled him under. It'll pull you under just like him." Ward paused, and studied the water between the boat and the shore. Thompson was right. Everyone stood in silence for a few minutes hoping the man would bob to the surface where they could reach him. But he never surfaced. With everyone else safely on the ground, the men removed their hats and watched as the boat went all the way over on its side and settled further down, with a loud hiss of escaping steam, until only about half of the pilot house and part of its stacks were showing above water.

By this time it was early evening, and Mr. Burwell, the man with the buckboard, stated he was taking the three women and two male passengers to his home and he invited Ward, Thompson and Peters to ride along as he felt sure his wife and daughter had enough food for a good, hot dinner for everyone. The three men took him up on his offer.

After a great meal and conversations around the table about where everyone was from, and how the five passengers had ended up unfortunately on the little batwing "Governor Lane," Ward and his two men unrolled their bedrolls and found sleep in Burwell's barn.

The next day the trio traveled for several miles on the old wagon road which paralleled the Richmond & Danville Railroad. The road intersected with the road that angled northeast to Ridgeton, and the men were anxious to get the news from three tattered soldiers they encountered around noon. Their story was similar to what they had heard from the other paroled soldiers the days before. One ex-soldier had a slightly different story. Ward noticed the man had no shoes, and his feet were wrapped with long, dirty rags. While they sat on some large rocks beside the road, the soldier, whose last name was Briggs, told the group:

"I was captured at Bentonville last month, and sent to a Yankee prison camp. It was a make-shift kind of fort which one of the guards said had been thrown together just for us prisoners from that battle. They were getting ready to ship us north to a larger prison camp, somewhere called Camp Chase. Before that could happen, they received word that Johnston had surrendered and the war was over. The captain who was over the guards, evidently drank a lot and really didn't want to be bothered with us. So he simply opened the gates and let us go! We first thought it was a set-up and once we got outside they would shoot us in the back for escaping. But as we went through, they were all drinking from a keg of whiskey with the captain and really celebrating. Seventeen of us just walked out and went our separate ways. I couldn't find the guard who had took my shoes, but I didn't care, I just wanted out of there!"

As he was telling his story, Peters was going through one of the large bags on the pack horse, and came back with a pair of beat up shoes. He said to Briggs, "These ain't the greatest, but they'll be better than your rags." Thompson appeared with an old pair of socks, and said, "Here put these on. Looks like I'll have to wash the pair I got on, after all!" Peters looked at Ward and pinched his nose, as each gave the other a knowing look.

They camped that evening along the road, and got an early start the next morning. The first few hours were uneventful. The trio passed a handful of paroled ex-Confederates who simply wanted a drink of water and then went on their way. In the afternoon, their road intersected the road that turned north. After Ward checked his compass and approved the turn, they soon recognized that road as the road that ran through Ridgeton and past the Anderson farm.

As they rode slowly through Ridgeton, Thompson remembered, "Seems just as dark and dirty as it was when we passed through it on our way to meet Governor Lane." There were few people on the streets, and the same ladies were watching them from the second floor balcony of the hotel, as on their earlier visit.

Anxious to see Stephens again and share their adventures since they had left him with the Andersons, the three picked up the pace to a good trot, and passed hurriedly through town.

## Chapter 16

The trio rode along in silence, until they turned off the main road into the lane to the Anderson's. Ward got a funny feeling as soon as they turned down the lane. The hairs on the back of his neck stood up. It was too quiet. He raised his clinched fist and the three halted. The only thing visible that kept the farm from appearing deserted was the gray horse tied to a ring in the side of the barn. No person was visible. They moved ahead slowly, with Ward dismounting and walking to the house, while Peters and Thompson rode to the barn, dismounted, and tied up the pack horse. Ward walked up on the front porch and listened for a few seconds. Hearing no sounds from inside, he knocked at the front door. Mr. Anderson answered the door after several seconds. He opened the front door, blinked several times, and said, "I figured it was you." By the cold way Anderson said the words, Ward sensed something was definitely wrong. By that time, Peters and Thompson had joined him on the porch. Anderson opened the door wide, and motioned for the three men to come inside. The first thing Ward noticed was that Stephens was nowhere in sight, and his little make-shift bed was just as they had left it. He looked around the two rooms, and looked back at Anderson, who was standing still and saying nothing. Mrs. Anderson was standing just inside the kitchen looking at them, with a solemn look on her face. Anderson said, finally, "Let's sit at the table." Ward knew then that something had happened to Stephens, he just couldn't guess what. Anderson took a deep breath, blinked three times, and started with, "Stephens is dead. He died saving our lives…"

Ward didn't hear the next few words. Anderson's mouth was moving, but Ward couldn't hear anything for the roar in his head. For an instant it was the thunder of cannon fire at Gettysburg, again. He gritted his teeth and forced himself back to reality.

Thompson and Peters were both almost yelling, "How? How did he die? What happened?" Anderson blinked four times, and in that space of time, he relived the last minute of Stephen's life, and again heard the muffled gunshot that ended the life of the intruder.

Anderson began by saying, "…It happened the day after you fellows left…" He slowly related the story of how the intruder had worked on their sympathies and got into the house and got a free meal, and in conversation Stephens had caught him in several lies about his military service. At that point the intruder had drawn his large knife and said he was going to kill all three of them. The three men looked at each other with astonishment. Anderson paused, caught his breath, and continued with a definite catch in his voice: "I looked around for a knife or some weapon, but just couldn't see one. I swear I would have fought him if I had had something. Stephens was lying on his bunk, covered in the old gray blanket. Stephens called the man a liar, challenged him to come closer, and fight someone his own age. When the intruder raised his knife and walked to Stephens to kill him first, Stephens shot him right through the blanket. The intruder raised his knife, and with his last breath, fell on Stephens, burying the knife in his chest. We tried to help Stephens but he was gone. They both died at the same time."

Ward had finally recovered and was able to talk and think coherently. "Were you two injured or hurt?"

Anderson lowered his head and answered, "No, thanks to your friend's quick thinking. We weren't sure what to do next, so we buried them both in the back yard, where our little baby is buried."

After another hour of questions from Ward, Thompson and Peters, with Anderson patiently trying to answer them, silence fell on the group. Ward looked at Thompson and Peters and said, "We have to notify his family, and tell them where Lige is buried."

Anderson added, "We gave him a Christian burial, and I said a few words over his grave. Lorena did some kind of Cherokee death chant, and that's all we knew to do."

Ward and the other two nodded in acceptance.

Ward said after another few minutes of silence, "Can we walk out back and see his grave?"

Anderson answered, "Certainly, follow me." Mrs. Anderson went back to work in the kitchen.

The four men walked out back, removed their hats, and stood over Stephens's grave. His gun belt was still hanging on the wooden cross. Anderson said, "That hump of dirt a few feet away is where we buried the intruder. I didn't say nothing over his grave." Anderson turned and walked back to the house.

After a few minutes of silence, Ward finally said, "Well, Lige, you always wanted to die as a hero in battle, so I guess you got your wish. The three of us and the Andersons will never forget the sacrifice you made to save two peoples' lives. May you rest in peace. It was an honor to serve with you." Ward saluted.

The other two mumbled, "Rest in peace."

Thompson looked at Ward, stepped over to the intruder's grave and spit on the pile of dirt. Peters simply smirked. Ward said nothing.

While walking back to the house, Ward stopped the other two and said, "I think Lige would want us to give at least part of his money that Governor Lane entrusted us with, to the Andersons." He waited for an opinion from Peters or Thompson. Peters thought for a moment and replied, "I think so, too." Thompson nodded his head in agreement. Ward went over to his horse, and pulled out the large leather pouch that contained their parole papers and the envelope with Lige's share of the money. He counted out $100 in U.S. currency. The three went back into the house where Anderson was sitting at the kitchen table. Ward sat down and said, "When we completed the mission we were sent on, the governor of North Carolina gave each of us a little money for the successful completion of the job. We all agree that Elijah Stephens would have wanted you to have part of it in return for all you did for him." He slid the $100 across the table to Anderson, who stared at it. Before he could object, Ward hurriedly added, "That's not half of his share, and we are going to deliver the rest to his family, but you certainly deserve this." Anderson thought for a moment, and with a heavy sigh, he accepted the bills.

"We buried him with the book he brought with him, you know." Anderson said.

The others looked surprised. Peters admitted, "We knew he could read a little, but never saw him reading a whole book."

Ward added, "That was the right thing to do."

Anderson added, "It was Dickens' *Great Expectations.*" He then looked down, and confessed, "I kept his gun. I hope you don't mind."

"Not at all. You might need it."

Anderson looked around and said, "Hey, where's your other fellow, that Wells fellow? He didn't also get killed did he?"

Peters chuckled and said, "No, when we heard the war was over, he just went home. We were already in North Carolina, and he said he was only about forty miles from his home."

Anderson suddenly straightened up and said, "I just remembered..." He walked over to the little bed where Stephens had spent his last hours, reached under it, and pulled out a set of saddlebags. He brought them back to the table, and placed them in front of Ward. "These are his things. If you are going to visit his family, please give this to them. It's just a few clothes, his razor, and a few other things.

119

But also in it is a letter he was writing to his mother. I didn't read it when I saw who it was to."

After another moment of silence, Peters said, "I would be proud to take his things and his share of the money and deliver it to his family. I go right through Giles County on my way home. I knew Lige better than anyone else, and they should hear the news from me." As Ward considered this idea, Peters added, "When I've given them the news, I'll write you and let you know, so you can send them a letter." Ward thought some more, and finally nodded his head in agreement. The three men were still in shock.

Mrs. Anderson brought over a hot pot of coffee she had been heating in the kitchen. With it were two chipped cups, and two dented tin cups. Anderson seemed to be comfortable with one of the tin cups. Mrs. Anderson went back to work in the kitchen, and Mr. Anderson poured his own, and passed the coffee pot to Ward and the others.
Ward had been silently debating within himself when they should leave. He finally said to Anderson, "After we finish our coffee, and water the horses, I think we'll head on toward home in Virginia."

Anderson, who had been staring off into space, replied "You know, with some of that money, I'm going to be able to buy a new plow or get our old one fixed." He smiled slightly, for the first time since the other three men had known him.

The men finished their coffee, said goodbye and expressed their thanks for the hospitality to Mrs. Anderson, and walked out to the horses. Mr. Anderson followed.
Each man led his horse around the barn to the watering trough, along with the pack horse. While the horses were drinking their fill, Ward put Stephens's saddlebags on the pack horse. Ward turned to Anderson and said, "We will let Lige's family know where he is buried, in case they want to come and take him home."

Anderson nodded, and said, "I was thinking the same thing."

Finally the three men were ready to ride. Peters and Thompson mounted. Thompson took the reins to the pack horse, and the two waited for Ward to say his goodbye to Anderson. He shook Anderson's hand, and said "I thank you for all you did for Lige Stephens and all your hospitality. Please thank your wife for us."

Anderson blinked a few times, as if looking for the right words. He finally said, simply, "Godspeed, major."

The three rode up the lane, and turned north on the road. They rode in silence for an hour or more. Ward's initial goal had been to make it to Falls Bluff that day, but they had left the Anderson's too late to make it all the way in daylight. When they reached the junction with the old cowpath they had traveled on their way south, Ward turned off into the path and found a clear spot among some trees. The thing that worried Ward was if the Rhode Island Yankee regiment was still blocking the main road ahead. He also commented to Peters and Thompson, "We certainly don't want to run into Stoneman and his cavalry, either." He decided they would wait until the next morning and scout ahead or stop at a house and ask someone if they thought the road was clear. They gathered a few sticks and pieces of dead wood for a small fire. Their conversation around the fire over their meager dinner was understandably subdued.

Union Army Gen. George Stoneman had been Stonewall Jackson's roommate when they were both at West Point, before the war. In the previous month, Stoneman had raided up into Virginia, then turned back down into North Carolina in April, where he raided and burned the prison for Union soldiers at Salisbury.

Ward asked, "Do either of you know just where Stephens's family lives in Giles County?"

Peters answered, "All I know is that he said he lived just a few miles from the county seat."

Thompson added, "That's more than I knew."

Peters concluded, "When I get there, I'll ask questions in the courthouse and around town. I'm sure I'll be able to find them."

Ward poked the fire with a stick, and watched the embers float upward toward the sky. Instead of thinking about the death of their friend, he made himself think about the pleasant greeting he hoped to receive at Falls Bluff.

## Chapter 17

The next morning after a short breakfast of some of the food given to them by Rosalee when they had left Owings Mill, Ward ordered Thompson, "Ride on ahead a mile or two and see if anyone can tell you about the road between here and Falls Bluff, especially if there are still any Union troops blocking the road."

Thompson saddled his horse and headed out on the road just after sunup. He only saw one farmer out by his barn and turned down his lane, and tipped his hat. He asked him what he knew about the safety of the road going north. The farmer shrugged, and said "I don't know nothing." He turned his back on Thompson and walked into his barn.

Back out on the road, Thompson was beginning to think about turning back, when he came upon a single walking soldier in a very worn Confederate uniform. He had the faded blue facings on his sleeves of an infantryman, and a corporal's stripes.

Thompson gave a casual salute, and said "Good morning, corporal. It looks like you've had your buttons cut off, so you must have been in the hands of the Yanks."

"Yeah. I left Appomattox about the 11th or 12th but only got a little ways, before a Yank patrol grabbed me up and took me at gunpoint to their camp. They were all looking to capture Jeff Davis and questioned me about what I knew, which was nothin'. "

"Do you know what regiment it was that captured you?"

"Yeah, I think it was a couple companies of the 14th Rhode Island Infantry."

Thompson chuckled, "We also had a brush with the other part of that bunch, about that time."

"They kept me for two days and never 'splained nothing. But their colonel received word that Jeff Davis had been captured somewhere down in Georgia. As soon as he got the word, he ordered the companies to break camp and they headed back north toward home. Fortunately they turned me loose, instead of shooting me."

"Do you know anything about where Gen. Stoneman and his cavalry are?"

"I heard some of the yanks talking that as soon as he burned the prison at Salisbury, he received the word of Davis's capture, and he also

122

headed back north. One of the yanks said Stoneman was really pissed when he couldn't free the yank prisoners at Salisbury, because they had been sent out somewhere else the day before he got there."

"So there aren't any yanks between here and Falls Bluff?"

"Right. The road is clear. You wouldn't have water in that canteen, would you?"

"Of course, here have a good swig."

The corporal took a long drink, thanked Thompson, and headed on up the road.

Thompson turned around and rode at a smooth gallop back to Ward and Peters to give them the good news.

With not having to take the cowpath which took them most of two days to traverse earlier on their way south, the three remained on the main road and made good time. Ward felt they could make it to Falls Bluff by evening if they were lucky. They only encountered two other paroled soldiers, both on horseback with the yellow facings on their sleeves signifying they were ex-Confederate cavalrymen. They related how they were lucky in that they had been allowed to keep their horses when paroled, and verified that the rest of the road was indeed clear to Falls Bluff. The three traveled at a comfortable trot, and arrived at Falls Bluff, late that afternoon.

As the three men rode through town, Ward smiled when he counted the days of the week and realized it was another Thursday afternoon. That meant that Delia should be hard at work on Friday's paper. He told Thompson and Peters, "Get a room at the hotel, I'll catch up with you later."

Thompson grinned and mumbled to Peters, "I'm not going to bet money on that." They split off and turned in at the hotel. Ward continued on and tied up in front of the newspaper office. It wasn't quite five o'clock and the door was unlocked. He walked in as the small bell tinkled over the door.

A voice from the back of the building yelled out, "I'll be there in a minute!"

Ward stood just inside the door with his hat in his hand. Delia must be in the back storeroom, he thought. He tried to swallow the big lump in his throat. She came out, wearing an ink-stained apron and walking quickly, until she saw who it was. She stopped. Ward said with a smile, "Just your lowly press man stopping by."

Delia took a second to find the words and finally also smiled and said, "I didn't know if I would ever see you again or hear from you. Then a few days ago, a weird looking little man pulls up in front with an

123

oddly made buckboard, and an ugly sneer on his face. He asked if I might be Mrs. Simmons. I thought it might be trouble." I replied, "Yes, I'm Mrs. Simmons, and who might you be?"

" 'It ain't important who I am.' He said, 'I come from Mr. Collins, the right hand man of Governor Lane of North Carolina.' "

"So what…I don't know a Mr. Collins or Governor Lane."

" 'Mr. Collins sends you a shipment I brung.' "

"You must have the wrong town, I never ordered anything from North Carolina."

"The weird little man produced a crumpled piece of paper, which he had to hold at arms' length to read, and said 'Mr. Collins said to tell you it was from a man named Ward.' "

"He got off the buckboard and motioned for me to come around to the back. He dropped the board on the tail end, and we looked into the back of the wagon, which appeared totally empty. I thought the little man was off in the head."

"He grinned and began tearing up the floor boards of the buckboard, to reveal a large hidden compartment, running the full length of the bed of the buckboard. In the compartment were three large stacks of blank newsprint paper covered with oil cloth."

"I told him I didn't have any money for that much paper, to which he replied that it 'had been taken care of by Mr. Ward.' "

"I finally gave in and accepted the strange delivery. I had Stonewall, who has been helping me around the newspaper, to come out and help the man unload the newsprint paper. I do appreciate the paper, and it came just in time. But how much do I owe you?"

Ward was quick to brush it off: "The Governor was going to burn it all up, along with his papers in his warehouse, and I just took it off his hands. It didn't cost me a cent."

Delia said, "I do appreciate it. It's just that usually when someone does a nice act they want something in return."

Ward replied simply and humbly, "I ask for nothing in return. I just wanted to help."

Both seemed unsure what to do or say next. Neither spoke a word, but looked unblinking into each other's eyes. Delia stepped forward, put both her hands softly on his arms, stood up on her tip toes, raised her face toward his, and closed her eyes. Ward swallowed hard, but took that as a message that a kiss would not be rebuffed. A kiss. A hesitant two second kiss, with both their bodies stiff and still unsure. Their lips parted. Without a word, or moving their feet, they kissed again. Something changed. This time it was several seconds longer, their bodies seemed to relax, and they melted further into each other's arms. An unspoken message passed between the two as their lips parted and they continued looking into each other's eyes. It was a feeling neither had experienced in the few years since losing a spouse. A single tear ran down Delia's cheek. She said, "I'm sorry. I'm still trying to determine if my Michael would approve of this."

After a few seconds, Ward responded, "When we lose someone we love very much, a part of us dies, as it did when my Helen died. But thinking about how thoroughly I knew her, I really do believe that she would approve if she could communicate with us. I never met your Michael, but I have to believe that if he loved you in the way you loved him, that he would also approve."

She nodded her head "yes," and hurriedly added, "I really do believe that both of them would want us to live a happy life."

They both smiled, and embraced fondly. They didn't need more words.

Ward removed his jacket and gun belt, rolled up his sleeves, and the two happily finished setting the type for Friday's paper, and inked the press. Both were obviously happy to be working together again, and enjoyed each other's company. When the printing was finished early the next morning, Ward took his horse and moved down to the hotel, where he found Peters and Thompson playing a friendly game of poker in their hotel room. They both seemed somewhat surprised to see Ward, but asked no questions.

After a few hours sleep, Peters arose first about eight a.m. and went downstairs for breakfast, and to see if there was a recent out of town newspaper anywhere. Ward, unlike his usual habit of being the first up, actually slept until after eight, when he came downstairs to inquire about paying for a bath, before he went back to the newspaper office. When he left, Thompson was still asleep. After washing off the trail dust, Ward entered the dining room to find Peters having coffee and reading a three day old newspaper.

Ward asked, "What's new in the paper?"

Peters related, "That fellow was right. President Davis was captured in Georgia. It appears they are taking him back up north maybe for a trial."

"They'd be better off if they just let him go. If they hang him it's just going to cause more bad feelings."

"The rest of the paper is just about the end of the war and the soldiers from both sides getting to go home."

Ward couldn't help but wonder if that paper Peters was reading wasn't where Delia got some of her news for happenings outside the county, to print in the *Falls Bluff Weekly*. He would have to ask.

Just as Ward was getting ready to leave, Thompson came down the stairs and joined them at their table. He grinned and remarked, "Didn't expect to see you up this early."

After a few minutes' pause, while Thompson ordered eggs and fried potatoes for breakfast, Ward continued, "I've been thinking and I think I'll stay here in town at least through today and not start out for Bedford County until maybe tomorrow. I don't want to hold you fellows up, so what do you want to do?"

Peters and Thompson looked at each other, and sheepishly looked at the floor, before Peters answered, "We were talking about that last night, and we figured maybe you were going to hang around here for awhile, so we are going to head straight home."

Ward nodded his head and added, "Don't blame you. You two can take the pack horse and figure out what to do with him later. But you should go by the newspaper office and give your regards to Delia before you head out."

The two agreed, and after another cup of coffee while Thompson finished his breakfast, the three walked together to the newspaper office. They were greeted by young Stonewall, who was loading his little wagon to take newspapers to the general store and a couple of other customers.

Ward smiled and extended his hand, "Hello, Stonewall. Great to see you again."

The young man grabbed Ward's hand and smiled and said, "Isn't it great the war's over, major? By the way, my given name is Aaron Phillips. We don't need to use secret names anymore."

"You're certainly right, Aaron Phillips. And you can call me Henry from now on."

Aaron then shook hands with Peters and Thompson, and each was jovial in his greetings.

Delia came from the back of the building, all cleaned up from the night's work and cheerful in a light yellow flowered dress. She smiled, said "Good morning!" and shook hands with Peters and Thompson, who thanked her again for rescuing them that first night they had been in Falls Bluff.

After the greetings, Ward said, "These two are going to head back today to their homes, and I do need to also go home to Bedford County and see my mother, and brothers and sister, but I'm not leaving until maybe tomorrow."

Delia nodded her head as she looked at Ward, "I figured you'd be leaving soon."

Thompson and Peters shuffled their feet during this awkward moment, and they took that opportunity to say their goodbyes, and they headed for the door. Ward said, "I'll help you load the pack horse and get things ready," and walked out with the two. He turned at the door and said, "I'll be back in a few minutes." Aaron headed out with his cart at the same time, and turned down the street.

Ward helped the other two get the horses from the stable and saddle them. He opened one of the large bags that was carried by the pack horse and extracted a spare shirt, socks and under drawers. When Peters and Thompson were ready to mount up, Ward said to them both that it had been an honor to serve with them and he wished them good luck and a happy life. They both returned the honor to serve. The two saluted him, he returned a casual salute, and shook their hands. He reminded Peters to write to him as soon as he found Stephens's family and delivered his share of the money. The two headed out of town and turned north. Ward carried his extra clothes back to the hotel room.

When Ward entered the newspaper office, he saw Delia sitting at the roll-top desk in the back of the large room. When he approached her, she quickly turned away from papers she had been looking at, and quickly wiped a tear. Ward, who had trained himself to notice details, caught the movement and asked her, "Delia, what's wrong?"

She turned back to the papers and said, "Nothing. It's nothing."

He lightly touched her arm and said, "I know better. I can tell it's something more than nothing. Perhaps I can help."

She thought about whether to say anything or not, and finally sighed and handed him the papers. "We have a new tax man in town who supposedly works for the county, but I think he's a Yankee that has been put in the job. He keeps sending notices that he is going to foreclose on the newspaper and my home, because I haven't paid the taxes in two years. It's ridiculous! Before the war, the taxes were less than ten dollars a year each on the business and the house, and now all of a sudden it's over fifty dollars for the newspaper and twenty dollars for my house for that two years. I'm afraid I don't have the money and there's nobody in town or the county that will loan money right now. So I don't know what I'm going to do." The last was followed by another tear on her cheek.

Ward slowly took the papers from her and read them carefully. He asked, "Did everyone's taxes go up like this?"

127

"I talked to Mr. Mills at the general store, and a couple of other business owners, and they all have the same problem."

"Where is this guy's office?"

"He has a small office in a corner of the general store."

"Let me go talk to him and see if he will grant an extension"

"I think you're wasting your time, but it's worth a try."

Ward took the tax papers and walked down the street to the hotel, where he went up to their room and retrieved his .44 Remington and counted money out of his saddlebag. He continued on to the general store, where he walked in, took his hat in his hand, adopted a timid and shy look, and approached the man sitting at a desk in the corner. He asked almost apologetically, "Are you the county tax man?"

The rotund gentleman looked over his glasses, and said, "Yes. My name's Malloy. State your business."

"I represent Mrs. Ardelia Simmons, who owns the local newspaper, and has received notices that you're about ready to foreclose on her property. How could we apply for an extension to give her a little more time?"

"I am not granting any extensions. She owes the taxes and that's the end of it."

"Perhaps not quite. I went through the back issues of the local newspaper for the last six months, and could find no official notice of a tax increase. Evidently you raised everybody's taxes in this area, and that's a tax increase. By Virginia law, you must post a notice of an increase in three successive issues of local newspapers around the county, which it appears you have failed to do."

"Now wait just a minute. We placed our notices in the Lynchburg newspaper."

"I don't believe there is a court in this area that would agree that that was a local newspaper. It's not in this county, and there's a weekly newspaper here in town. I think we might take you to court on that point."

"I doubt you would succeed in that. By the time the case would get on a court docket, we will control most of the judges and you'll lose."

"Well, Mr. Malloy, it seems we are stuck in the mud. Here's how we are going to resolve it. Here are seventy dollars in U.S. currency to pay Mrs. Simmon's taxes in full, and I want your signed receipt stating that."

Malloy fell back as if he had been punched, and growled: "I don't think I can write a receipt like that, without examining the tax books all over again."

Ward smiled and said, "No, you are going to write the receipt in the next five minutes." With that, he unbuttoned his coat, and checked the pocket watch in his vest pocket. Of course when the coat opened, it revealed the handle of his Remington sticking out of his belt. He smiled and stared Malloy straight in the eyes and said, "Now write it."

Malloy's hands began to shake, but he took his pen and wrote the receipt, which he unsteadily handed to Ward.

Ward read it carefully, and folded it and put it in his coat pocket. He stood abruptly and said to the little man, "Now what you are going to do is place a paid notice in the next three issues of the *Falls Bluff Weekly* explaining your tax increase. In the meantime, I will encourage all the business owners to unite and march on the courthouse in protest, and we'll see how the county government likes it."

He turned abruptly and walked out, as the little man drew a dirty handkerchief and wiped the sweat from his face.

On his way back to the newspaper, Ward hesitated at the hotel door, and decided to go back up to his room and drop off his Remington, thinking Delia would certainly have noticed it stuck in his belt and would want to know how it had figured in the meeting with the tax man.

She was waiting for him when he entered the newspaper office. She tried to read his face, and finally said, impatiently, "Well? Did we get an extension?"

"Better than that. It's taken care of." Ward said as he handed her the paid in full receipt. Then he added, "You are also going to get a prepaid notice from the tax man to go in the next three issues of the newspaper."

She studied the receipt and then questioned him, "So what happened? He didn't strike me as someone who would just give in to your boyish charm."

Finally cornered, Ward admitted, "I paid both taxes and threatened him with a march on the county courthouse, if he didn't put a proper legal notice in your paper."

She looked at the floor, and said in a meek voice, "Thanks, of course, because I couldn't figure how I would pay it. It is a relief. But, now I am beholden' to you."

He took her gently by both arms and said, "No, you aren't. The governor of North Carolina gave each of us some money for the mission we did in delivering some papers to him, and so I simply put some of it to this good use."

Without a reply, she leaned forward and embraced him, and the embrace was mutual. They stood that way, intertwined, for a long minute.  Ward felt a warm feeling that he hadn't felt since Helen had passed away.  Delia didn't say anything, but from the look on her face, felt the same thing.

She suddenly sprang back a little, and looked up at him with a smile, and said, "I know what I can do! It won't mean much to you, because you're leaving, but I will make you a partner in the *Falls Bluff Weekly!*"

"If you're sure that's what you want to do, I won't argue. And as for my leaving – yes, I am going back to Bedford County to see my mother and brothers and sister. But I now have a reason for coming back here, and if everything is alright there, with my sister and brother-in-law running the farm, and if they plan to stay with mother, then I feel like I'm free to be here.  I hope to be gone no more than two weeks."

"Good.  Because I need the new partner to organize the papers and files.  I tried to keep up for the first few months, but finally gave up, and just let them pile up on the desk."

He laughed and said he had noticed the stacks of letters and other papers that had accumulated.  She invited him to sit at the desk and see what he could do.  They both sat down at the desk and talked.  He realized she did not know about the death of Stephens, and he had just then thought of it.  He explained what had happened to Stephens, and how they had left him with the Andersons, while the others went on to complete their mission.  He related with a lump in his throat about how Stephens had died saving the lives of the old couple.  He concluded with, "I just realized that Wells doesn't know about Stephens," because he had headed home from Owings Mill, before Ward and the others had traveled to the Andersons.  He asked, "Is there any blank sheets of paper anywhere in this desk? I'll write Wells a letter to let him know." After writing the letter, Delia showed him how she had more or less organized the papers in the past. She had a fantastic memory in that she could recall almost all the letters and papers and their significance, if any. She admitted that she did get some news from the days-old papers that made it into the town and reprinted them in their paper.  She explained that it was a normal procedure for small town newspapers. With a sigh, she expressed the hope that with the war over, they would get a telegraph office in town and she could get more up to date news that way.

They spent the rest of the day just enjoying each other's company and talking about the problems of the small town newspaper, in general, and those of the *Falls Bluff Weekly* in particular. They sat and wrote an editorial together for the next week's paper regarding the tax situation in the county.

When it neared closing time, Delia invited Ward to her house for a home-cooked meal. Of course he accepted.

They walked together up the street to her little house. Delia put on her apron and went into the kitchen, and asked Ward: "Why don't you build us a little fire in the fireplace while I cook?"

Ward found a few small pieces of wood and piled them in the fireplace grate and got the fire going. He put in one larger piece of wood, dusted off his hands, and looked around the living room. It was tastefully furnished, if a little sparse. He went to the bookshelf, and looked over a group of small books on the first shelf, between two old bookends. He was surprised to find they were school books: two *McGuffey's Readers*, a book of *Primary Bible Questions for Young Children* by Roct, a *Ray's Arithmetic*, and a *Confederate First Reader* by Mrs. Moore. Most interesting was the *Geographical Reader for Dixie Children*. He was thinking that it was odd for Delia to have these books in her small library, if she had no children, when she said from just behind him, while wiping her hands on her apron, "In case you are wondering, I was a replacement school teacher here the first year Michael and I were married. That geography has a few hand-colored maps that both myself and the school children always found interesting."

Delia warmed up some salt-dried pork, vegetables, and made fresh biscuits, and opened a jar of blackberry jellies. It was the most wonderful meal Ward had had since the start of the war.

# Chapter 18

Following the meal, the two sat in front of the fire, about six feet apart. After a brief conversation about other happenings of the day, a period of companionable silence ensued. Delia dusted off the front of her dress, which stirred up a small tuft or flake of cotton. She examined it, and with a grin, gently blew it in Ward's direction. He at first wasn't sure how to respond, but he eventually blew it back in her direction. She chuckled and said, "So I see you have played 'Cotton Flies.'"

Ward answered, "We tried to play it at home with feathers, but they wouldn't go straight."

The two were able to pass the tuft between them a few more times, before Ward blew it too quickly, and it went off course, floated down, and landed. So he lost. Delia added, "It's really funny when someone accidentally sucks it in their mouth, and tries to blow it back out." They both chuckled as they envisioned that happening.

After a few minutes, Delia mentioned another game: "I also remember 'I Love my Love with an A.' Did you ever play that one?"

After thinking for several seconds, he answered, "I saw my sister and some of the other young ladies play that, before the war."

"Let me explain it. One person begins with the letter 'A' by saying 'I love my love with an A, because he is agreeable, and his name is Andrew." Then the other player answers with: 'I love my love with a B, because she is beautiful, or she lives in Biloxi.'"

"I remember it now," he said.

"Let's start it this way: I loved my love with an A, because he was affectionate and he was from Amelia."

Ward took the past tense to mean she was thinking of her deceased husband, Michael.

After some thought, he looked away and replied, "I love my love with a B, because she is beautiful and from Bedford."

Delia took his looking away to mean he was thinking of his lost wife, Helen.

She came back quickly with, "I love my love with a C, because he was charming, and he is from Clarke County."

Just as quick, and getting into the rhythm, Ward responded, "I love my love with a D, because her name is Delia…"

She gasped and put her hand to her mouth.

Ward wanted to take it back, but it was too late.

She covered her face with her hands and breathed two heavy sighs.

He blurted, "I didn't mean that the way it sounded, it was the only word I could think of that started with a D, and…"

She didn't let him finish. Still holding her face in her hands, she was crying. She finally said, "I think you should leave."

He made one more attempt, "But I meant…"

"Just go!"

He gave up in astonishment, picked up his hat and, with one look back, turned and walked out the door. He walked slowly back to the hotel, where he stopped in the saloon and had a few stiff whiskeys, which only made him half sick. He went to his room, dropped on his bed, facing the ceiling. He relived the evening, thinking how happy it had begun. The little games must have reminded her too much of Michael. The rest of his night was spent with *What do I do now?* running through his whiskey-affected mind.

After laying awake most of the night, staring at the ceiling, he got up early in the morning, when the dining room opened. After a quick breakfast, and some black coffee, he decided what to do. He checked out of the hotel, walked to the stable, saddled his horse and stuffed a napkin containing half his breakfast in his saddle bags. He would get out of town and finally get to see his mother. As he rode slowly past the newspaper office, he noticed two lanterns burning in the office, one of which had been placed on the front window sill. He was sure it had not been there before. He stopped in the middle of the street. After a full minute of indecision, he turned Andy toward the newspaper building and tied him up at the hitching post. *Now what?* He thought. *What do I say? Maybe if I make a full apology…*

With a deep breath, he took hold of the door knob and slowly turned it. To his surprise, it was unlocked and he opened the door. Delia was standing inside, about four feet from the door, as if she was expecting someone. With his hat in his hand, and a lump in his throat, he started with, "I want to apologize for…" Then they both realized that they had started in unison with exactly the same words, at exactly the same time. They both stopped.

She was quicker, with: "I'm sorry I went to pieces. I had held it all back ever since Michael's death and it just all came gushing out last

133

night. I had relaxed and let my guard down. I had no right to take it out on you. I'm very sorry." She looked down.

He replied with, "I should have been more thoughtful, but I did mean what I said for my letter D, and I still mean it."

She thought for a moment, looked up, and said, "I know, and I do care about you also. I just need some time to clear my head and pull myself back together. I figured you were heading to see your family in Bedford today. So please come back and we'll figure this whole thing out, together...you are coming back, aren't you?"

"Yes, of course. But I really do need to go to Bedford. I'll try to be back in two weeks."

She took his hand and squeezed it, and he decided to risk a slight, quick kiss on her hand. She did smile, at least, and said, "Now get on your way, or I'm likely to have another sob." He smiled, breathed a sigh of relief, and with a good feeling mounted Andy and headed briskly out of Falls Bluff. It was Saturday morning. Delia blew out the two lamps, locked the newspaper door and headed back home. She felt a desperate need to write a letter to her mother. Before she got home, she stopped suddenly, and asked herself: *Am I falling in love?*

The Ward ancestral home.

Ward exclaimed: "Thank God, it's still there!"

## Chapter 19

Ward rode along, deep in thought. He was reliving last night's conversation and this morning's parting with Delia. Her emotional reaction to their impromptu word game of the night before had surprised him. It was the first time he had seen her emotional side. But he felt better after this morning's talk, and remembered the firm grip of her hand on his. He thought: *So, where is this going to lead?* He smiled and hoped he knew the answer.

As he made the turn on the road that brought him parallel to the river, he noticed the layer of fog that was hanging over the river, bank to bank. It was like a thick blanket of cotton. In the passing of another mile it had crept over the bank and was edging onto the road. By then he could see that it had a slight swirl as it moved over the road, and it was thick. In the next mile the fog had not only covered the road but made it look like his horse was wading through it. As the fog grew deeper and rose to the horses' underbelly, he slowed to a very slow walk. It increased to a layer three or four feet deep. Andy became skittish, not understanding what this mess was that engulfed them. In another half mile it completely encompassed horse and rider. The odd thing that Ward noticed was how it muffled the roar of the river, which he had heard distinctly before. For the next few hundred yards of riding in the fog, the horse must have been able to see the road, or somehow sense how to stay on it. Ward felt the hairs bristle on the back of his neck. He stopped. Silence. He heard a clip-clop of a horse behind him and over his left shoulder. Then that horse stopped. Silence again. Ward slowly drew his Remington and held it in his lap. He turned slowly and looked over his left shoulder. Nothing but white cotton. Instead of swinging his horse around, he pulled back on the reins and the well-trained animal backed up four or five feet. He could see through the thick fog just the outline of the other horse and was able to tell it was riderless. It snorted and was obviously skittish, like his own mount. Ward listened carefully for any other sounds that would reveal where the rider might be. Total silence, except for the sounds of the horse breathing. He dismounted slowly, and as quietly as possible. With pistol at the ready, he walked back to the horse. He saw it had been an army horse, and had the typical army saddle, with a bedroll tied on the back. He petted its neck gently, which seemed to settle it somewhat. He carefully walked back behind the animal, searching intently for any sign of movement. Nothing. He walked a few more feet behind the horse and there, in a somewhat thinner patch of fog, he could see the dark form of a man lying motionless in the road. Ward, careful and alert for an ambush, took two steps closer to the man, and cocked his Remington. He now stood almost over top of the man, with his pistol pointed directly at him. The prone figure was unmoving. Ward knelt slowly over him and could see no wounds or evidence of injury, but he was unconscious. Ward drew his Bowie knife, held it under the man's nose, and could see a small cloud of moisture on the blade, showing that the man was breathing. The man's hat was lying beside him. Ward picked it up, noticing it was most likely a Confederate cavalryman's hat. On the front of it was the faded outline of where a hat insignia had been, which appeared to have been the crossed swords of a cavalry officer. Ward carefully nudged the man in the ribs with his revolver. No movement. He punched him a second time, and the man's eyes popped open, and he gasped as if waking from a deep sleep.

He sat bolt upright and said in a firm, commanding voice, "SIR, WE COULD NOT CAPTURE THE GUNS. WE WERE REPULSED AT THE ENTRENCHMENTS, SIR!"

Ward took hold of the man's arms and said gently, "Easy, soldier, the war's over. There isn't any more fighting."

The man looked at Ward as if seeing him for the first time. He then looked all around them, and asked: "Are we in Heaven or Hell?"

Ward chuckled and replied, "I think we are somewhere in between."

After another couple of deep breaths, the man seemed to regain his strength and awareness. He slowly said, "I must have fallen off my horse. I haven't slept in two days, and must have dozed off."

Ward asked, "Have you had anything to eat, how about a drink of water?"

"I don't remember the last time I ate, and I could sure use a bite of food."

Ward walked back to his horse and retrieved his canteen and a biscuit he had saved from breakfast. The man remained seated squarely in the middle of the road. He ate the biscuit and took a few drinks of water, and thanked Ward repeatedly for being a "good Samaritan." He asked Ward where he was headed.

Ward answered, "Heading home to Bedford County."

"I'm headed to Campbell County, which is right next door."

138

"We could ride along together, until the road forks."

"That would be good. If we talk maybe it will keep me awake."

The two men rode along and soon the fog cleared. The man's name was Perkins, and he had been an officer in a Virginia cavalry regiment from Campbell County. Both had been at Gettysburg, and compared their remembrances of the great battle. After several minutes of silence, Perkins began again, "We were in the cavalry battle on the third day, near the Rummel Farm. After we retreated, I was riding back over the battlefield, and there at my feet were two soldiers I had known since boyhood, from Campbell County, dead and staring straight up at the sky. I can't get that out of my mind."

Ward tried to tell the man that he also had similar memories, and agreed that "We probably won't ever forget those faces."

After a couple of hours, they came to a fork in the road. Perkins pointed out the right fork going to Lynchburg and Campbell County, and the left to Bedford County. The two men shook hands, and Perkins headed up the right fork and Ward continued on the left toward home.

As evening neared, Ward found a nice spot under three trees, only a few feet from the road. He gathered some dead limbs and built a small fire. He ate what was left of his food. It was a pleasant, warm evening. As he lay on his bedroll, looking up at the stars, he thought of Delia, and what he would find at his mother's. He drifted off into a peaceful, sound, sleep.

Ward was up soon after daylight, wanting to get an early start, in the hope that he could make it home to Bedford County before evening. He shared his water with Andy, refilled his canteen, and they headed back out onto the road.

Ward was anxious to see his mother again. She was not young at the age of fifty-four, but was still able to manage the farm and the house. (He hoped.) His younger brothers, Noah and Jonathan, had avoided the brunt of the war, and had been able to stay near home. His sister, Rachel, and her husband, Matthew Grimes, had moved in with their mother when Henry had gone off to war. He tried to remember something about Matthew, but all he could remember was that he was much older than Rachel, probably about fifty. He had dodged conscription into the Confederate Army due to a hip wound he had received while serving in the Mexican War that had left him with a noticeable limp. His mother had written Henry that sometime in late 1864, after Lincoln had freed the slaves, two ex-slaves who were escaping a cruel master in Georgia, stopped on their way north, at the house for a drink of water. They were a middle-aged father, and his teenaged son.  They offered to do a few chores for food for a day or two, and they had ended up staying to work on the farm in exchange for food, board, and an honest wage.

The closer he got to his home place, the more he worried: *What if the home he had known and loved wasn't even there anymore?* He had heard of some homes being burned in Bedford County by renegade Yank foraging parties. *What if they had burned his home, and his family hadn't known how to get a letter to him.  What if one of them had been hurt...or even worse.  What if....* He snapped out of it and looked forward to seeing his family again.

He kept riding all day, stopping only once to fill his canteen and for Andy to drink from the stream.

Late in the afternoon, he came to the familiar fork in the road at Benson's store.  He swallowed hard; the store that he had known and enjoyed since a small boy, was boarded up and abandoned.  But he took the fork toward home, and picked up the pace.  Finally a chill ran down his back as he rounded the last curve before home.  But as he rounded the curve, he said out loud: "Thank God, it's still there!"  His house was still there, the yard neat and clean, with a few roses blooming.  The barn was open and a horse inside shuffled its hooves.

As he turned in at the house, the front door opened, and a bald-headed man stepped out on the porch, and stared for a few seconds at him, then stuck his head back inside and yelled something at someone inside the house. As Ward got closer, he realized the man was Matthew Grimes, Rachel's husband. By the time he was dismounting, a gray-haired woman stepped out with Grimes, wiping her hands on an apron. His mother recognized him with a short yelp of "Henry, you're home!" At that instant, Rachel and his brothers, Noah and Jonathan, came out on the porch.  The others all held back for a few moments, as Henry dismounted and embraced his mother, and their reunion was a joyful one. She was shaking but almost laughing. She said "I only received your letter yesterday, but we were all full of hope that you were on your way." As Ward carried on this conversation with his mother, he couldn't help but glance at the little knoll off to their left, in a grove of trees.  It was where Helen was buried, along with his father.  After hugs from the other family members, Jonathan took Andy to the barn, and Ward unbuckled his gun belt and hung it on a rack inside the front door. His mother said, "I noticed you looking toward the graves on the knoll.  Are you going to talk to Helen?"

Ward replied, "Yes, there's something important I need to tell her."

"Then let me cut a few flowers for you to put on her grave."

While his mother gathered the flowers, Ward was introduced to Jonas and Jacob, the two freed slaves who were now paid workers for the family. Jonathan and Noah were both anxious to hear about Ward's adventures. They listened intently while Ward recounted his exploits during the war. He gave few details about his last mission into North Carolina. When his mother came back in the house, she had cut a few beautiful, small roses and peonies, and tied them together with a red ribbon.

Ward took the flowers and walked up the knoll and stood silently for a moment looking at the small stone that marked Helen's resting place. Finally he said, "Hello, wonderful wife. I have not forgotten you. Sometimes in the heat of battle and with bullets flying, it helped calm me to think of your smile and our brief time together. I will never feel for another what I felt with you, and the life we shared. You were taken from us way too soon. But I have met someone who makes me happy and I need to feel that you would approve of me getting to know her better. I feel that I know your spirit and that you would want me to find happiness again. Her husband was killed in the war, and she wrestled with her emotions about if he would approve, and has resolved herself to the fact that he would have." He stopped and just stood still for a few minutes. A voice from Heaven did not sound, nor did an apparition in a long gown appear. But what did happen that interrupted the complete silence, was a small, blue bird that lit on the bottom tree limb just behind the grave. Its beautiful song reached into Ward's deepest soul, and he felt a level of relief, and a strange warmth came over him. He took it to be what he had been waiting for. He knew he had his answer. He pressed two fingers to his lips and planted the kiss on her stone. He laid his flowers just in front of the stone, and stood for another minute near his father's resting place. He made his way slowly back to the house.

After a wonderful family dinner, Ward and his mother went into the small drawing room, off the front hallway. He asked her first how it was working out with Rachel and her husband living there and helping with the farm. She answered, "It has worked out well. And with Jonas and Jacob, we get along just fine." Ward listened carefully for any hint that that was not the case, but heard nothing that caused him to question her words.

Ward asked, "Has there been any talk about Rachel and Michael leaving now that the war is over?

"They said they are perfectly content here with our arrangement, and are happy to stay on if it agrees with me. But what are your plans?"

Ward squirmed and thought a moment before answering, "Of course I am prepared to stay if you need me, but something has happened. I have met a wonderful lady who runs the Falls Bluff newspaper. Her husband was killed at Cloyd's Mountain. She saved my life and that of Peters one night when we were in a pinch. I helped take care of her taxes on the newspaper and her home, and in turn, she made me a partner in the newspaper. I have helped her twice print the newspaper. We get along well, and we have briefly embraced." He paused, waiting for a response from his mother.

"Well, she sounds like a wonderful person. Do you want to go back to Falls Bluff?"

"Yes, I do. I feel like she and I left things up in the air, because I didn't know what I would find here."

She interrupted, "Well, put your mind at rest about us. Feel free to go back to Falls Bluff. The farm is recovering from being ravished by the war, and I am still healthy enough to help with the work. Thank God. You should probably discuss this with Rachel and Michael and your two brothers, but I feel like they will agree. And I know Helen would have wanted you to be happy. "

Ward nodded his head in agreement. He added, "I want to stay a few more days, regardless. Have there been any tax problems with the farm, or any other business problems I should look into? Myself and the squad were paid a few U.S. dollars for this last mission, and I will leave you most of my share to help out."

She replied, "We were able to pay the taxes, thank Heaven. But you need to talk to Matthew and Jonathan, who have been talking with a Mr. Willenhall, who came from England. He has been paying a few dollars rent to live in the little cabin your father built down in the trees, in the lower forty. He has offered to buy outright the lower forty acres the cabin is on. I don't know what to think of that. So please talk to Matthew and Jonathan, as Willenhall seems anxious."

When they finished their talk, Ward went out on the porch and talked with Matthew, Rachel, and Jonathan and Noah. They reinforced his mother's statement that they were indeed successfully keeping up the farm, and had no problem with the current arrangement. Matthew explained that Willenhall had indeed made a generous offer for the forty acres. He added, "I don't know where this fellow got his money, but he says he will not need a note or loan, and he will be paying in U.S. dollars. He did mention that he has slipped in and out, through the blockade back to England three times in the last few years. But he has never mentioned if he has a profession. He said he would be at the cabin for the next few weeks, so we could go down there in the morning and discuss this with him."

After that conversation, they all sat and enjoyed the peace and quiet for a good while, with the only sounds being a few crickets. Later, Ward felt very calm and satisfied, sleeping in his old room. Jonathan went sound to sleep in the other bed across the room, just as when they had been boys.

## Chapter 20

After breakfast the following morning, Ward and Matthew walked down over the back pasture to the small cabin on the "lower forty." A wisp of smoke was rising from the stone chimney. Willenhall's horse was loose in a small corral beside the cabin, carefully watching the approaching men. The man came out the front door, and waited for the two to dismount. Matthew made the introductions, and Willenhall and Ward shook hands firmly. Willenhall was a tall, lean man, with dark hair, a dark mustache, and a pair of deep, black, eyes. The three went inside and sat at the small kitchen table. After exchanging pleasantries, Ward asked with a grin, "I hear you have made it through the blockade a few times?"

Willenhall's reply, also with a grin, was simply, "Some blockade ship captains have been known to accept a bribe. They are in it for the money." He then explained that he had belonged to a secret group in England that had worked to raise money for the Confederacy.

Euston Willenhall IV had moved in the highest circles of power in Great Britain during the war. Two of his close business associates were Lord Haliburton and Lord Robert Cecil, the 3d Marquis of Salisbury. They were members of Parliament and were secret members of a group known as the Southern Independence Association, which supported the Confederacy. This group worked to raise funds to support the Confederate cause. With chapters in London, Manchester, and Liverpool, they had a larger support among the most powerful families in Great Britain than most people realized.

Willenhall looked carefully at Ward, with his dark eyes boring through him. He said, "Since the war is over, I'm going to tell you some things that I feel I can trust you with. Part of what our group did in London was to raise enough money to purchase several government bearer bonds. In one bazaar we held in Liverpool last October, we raised £21,000 pounds. We sent the packet of bonds by courier across the ocean and through the blockade to give to your President Davis. I wonder what happened to them?"

Ward smiled slightly, and said: "Mr. Willenhall, I understand from someone close to President Davis that the bonds were put to good use, and escaped the hands of the Yankees."

Matthew said nothing while this exchange occurred. He would ask Ward later what it all meant.

Ward brought the discussion back to the purchase of the forty acres. He asked, "If we were to sell, what are your plans for the property. You don't strike me as a dirt farmer."

Willenhall chuckled, and replied, "You are right about that. I want to build a roomy, but simple home, so I can bring my wife and mother over here to live with me. I'm not sure how they will be regarded in England, now that the Confederacy has expired, and our names are now public as having supported it. I don't think it will be safe for me to return in the near future. I was a barrister in England, and may open a small law office in town at some later date."

Ward nodded his head in understanding. They spent the next hour going over the details of the land purchase. Willenhall said Jonathan had walked him around where he thought the property lines were supposed to be, and he thought there had been a survey of some kind but hadn't seen it. Ward knew that might be the next challenge: finding someone who would survey. Ward mentioned that he needed to ride to the county courthouse, and see what the deed said, and if a survey had been filed.

Before they parted, Willenhall said, "I understand that your mother may be hesitant to let the land go. Do you think it would help if I said I was willing to go as high as $25 an acre?"

Ward did the multiplication in his head, and said: "You do realize that would make it $1,000... are you sure?"

Willenhall replied that he was sure, and would pay in U.S. dollars without a delay.

Ward was somewhat speechless, and so they ended the meeting with him stating that he would immediately discuss it with his mother and his brothers and sister.

After leaving Willenhall, they walked back to the main house and found his mother entertaining two neighbor ladies in the drawing room, so the two went back out to help Jonathan and Noah with repairs to the side fence.

That evening, after dinner, Ward explained to everyone, with some interjected comments from Matthew, Willenhall's offer. The others gasped when they heard the offer. His mother asked if he thought it was for real, or some kind of trickery. Ward assured them that this man was sincere, and he felt sure he had the money. Noah and Jonathan chimed in that it sure would help with some things they needed for the farm, such as a replacement for the plow, which was being held together by a splint and bailing wire, and that they really could use a work horse or mule. Matthew reminded Mrs. Ward about the repairs to the barn that had become necessary. After a few more minutes of discussion, Ward and his mother agreed for him to go to the courthouse and see what papers needed to be drawn up.

The following morning, Ward saddled up Andy and rode into the county seat, about ten miles from his home. He entered the courthouse at the Bedford County seat in mid-morning. After familiarizing himself with the organization of their records, he proceeded to research the records on the home place. His mother had told him that his father had drawn up a will that simply left everything to her alone. He had taken this intelligent action when he realized how serious his illness was. Ward found that will in the will books, and it was simple and straightforward. That was one load off of Ward's mind. His mother had inherited legally, and therefore she was the only one who needed to sign a deed. He next found the deed where his father and mother had purchased the land about 15 years earlier. Both their names were on the deed, so the legal ownership was without question. It took a little longer to work through the survey records, as they were organized differently from deeds and wills. But, sure enough, before his father's death, he had had Mr. Mansfield survey the lower forty acres and another plot of fifty acres next to it. Ward would have to ask his mother why the two surveys. But he copied the survey details into his notebook, as it gave the markers of the boundary lines. He would need that to prepare a legal deed. He rode home, and while sitting at his father's old rolltop desk, wrote out two copies of the new deed between his mother and Willlenhall, referencing the earlier survey. That evening, Ward sent Noah down to Willenhall's cabin, to inform him that they were ready with a new deed, and would like to meet and finish everything up at the house, the following morning. Willinhall informed Noah that he would be there, with the money, as agreed.

At exactly nine o'clock the following morning, Willenhall rode up to the house and tied up his horse. He knocked on the door, and was admitted by Matthew. After the usual greetings, the group seated themselves in the drawing room. Ward explained about the survey and that it had followed the exact lines that Jonathan and Willenhall had paced off previously, and that the deed repeated those lines exactly. Willenhall agreed and opened his leather dispatch pouch, and counted out $1,000 in U.S. fifty and twenty dollar bills. Ward looked carefully at the bills, and observed that some were relatively new and others old and worn, as one would expect. Ward then showed his mother where to sign the deeds, and Matthew and Jonathan signed as witnesses. Ward sat at the rolltop desk, and wrote out a receipt for the money paid, and noted that the amount was paid in full. After sealing the deal with handshakes all around, Rachel appeared with a large tray of small brandy glasses and small cookies. At the conclusion, Willenhall excused himself saying he wanted to go ahead and ride into the county seat and record the dead at the courthouse. The Wards, excited about this windfall, carefully set aside portions of the money for the two most pressing needs: a new plow, and another work animal, either a horse or mule. Ward's mother said she would like to have a few new plates, and a larger pan for the kitchen. Ward cautioned them all about showing too much cash in town. He suggested they deposit the rest in the county bank.

Reluctantly the group dispersed to take care of necessary chores. Ward began to think about what he was going to do next. He felt guilty in that he was thinking about getting back to Falls Bluff.

That evening, following dinner, Ward and his mother sat out in the rockers on the front porch. After more talk about what they needed to do about some house repairs, they both became quiet.

Ward felt torn between staying longer with her and his brothers and sister, and returning to Falls Bluff, to see Delia again, and with a choke, expressed his predicament.

Ward's mother walked over to him, took both his hands in hers and said, "Now listen to me! I am the luckiest mother in Bedford County. All my family survived the terrible war. Some families lost two or three men; but all my sons made it through. It has been a real blessing that Noah, Jonathan, and you made it through alive and are here now. Every mother expects her children to grow up, find jobs away from home, or get married and move away. But for the near future, Noah, Jonathan and Rebecca are here with me. Your life has taken you hundreds of miles away, and in the midst of the killing and bloodshed you have met someone wonderful. Go be with her and explore your feelings for each other and decide what you are going to do. Just please write to me whenever you can. I think the mail will be working reliably in a few more weeks." She took a deep breath, "My thoughts and prayers will go with you."

Ward hugged her and immediately felt a lot better.

The next day was taken up with a trip into the county seat. Ward and his mother road on the buckboard, and Jonathan and Noah rode their horses. It was a happy day in that for the first time since the start of the war, the family could purchase some needed groceries, without worry, and see if there was a plow to be found. Ward had Jonathan and his mother deposit some of the cash they had received from Willenhall in the county bank. It was one of the few banks that had remained open in that part of Virginia. Jonathan reported that there wasn't a plow for sale in the county seat, but Mr. Colbern, the owner of the general store, ordered one for them from Lynchburg.

After dinner that evening, Ward discussed his immediate plans with the family. The next morning he would head back to Falls Bluff. They all smiled at that, understanding he wanted to see Delia and settle things. Later he took Jonathan and Matthew aside, and in a low tone asked them both to keep an eye on Willenhall and what he did with the forty acres. "While he came across with the money as promised, I just don't trust him completely," he said. Matthew immediately agreed and added that the guy "makes my skin crawl."

The next morning, anxious to get started, Ward saddled Andy and collected some food in a sack, offered by his mother. He hugged each one and shook hands with Matthew, assuring all that he would write soon and let them know how things went in Falls Bluff.

It was a bright, sunshiny day, and Andy seemed to enjoy picking up the pace to a brisk trot. Ward found himself reminiscing about the camaraderie his squad had shared while riding together. It was a camaraderie born out of battle and war. He remembered Lige Stephens and the little cross in Anderson's back yard that marked his resting place. He had died saving the lives of others. That evening, after he made a small campfire and ate some of his mother's cornbread and cold chicken, he thought over and over again about what to say to Delia. On the one hand, he wanted to spit it all out and say he loved her deeply and that he would follow his mother's advice which had been to "follow your heart." But he was a little fearful of going too far, too fast, and maybe scaring Delia. Could he find an in-between path? But he was happy with the status of things with his mother and the farm, and was satisfied that they would manage just fine without him. That was a great relief. He fell asleep on his bedroll, thinking of Delia and their first kiss.

When morning came, he led Andy down to the stream and he waded in and washed off, before filling his canteen and heading out on the road. He was hoping desperately that Delia would care about him like he cared about her. He decided that no matter what she said, he would tell her how he felt.

He rode slowly into Falls Bluff about 2 p.m., and the town was busy. He tied up his horse at the newspaper office, dusted off his clothes, and as he entered the door to the tinkle of the little bell, he removed his hat. Again he had the lump in his throat. He was greeted by

148

Aaron Philips, who was setting type, with a friendly, "Mr. Ward, you're back!"

Ward nervously replied, "Good to see you again, Stonewall…I mean Aaron."

"Mrs. Simmons is in the back, I'll go get her."

Aaron went into the back storeroom; there were a few seconds of dreadful silence, before they both came back to the front. Before either could say anything, Aaron said, with a grin, "I'll go to the general store and see if Mr. Mills needs any more newspapers."

She approached Ward, face to face, and he began talking at a faster than normal rate, "I had a wonderful visit with my family, and am happy that they are getting along fine with running the farm without me. We were able to sell off forty acres for cash, and they have some money to buy things needed for the farm, and…."

Delia said something, softly.

Ward stopped in mid-sentence, and said, "I'm sorry, what did you say?"

She took one step closer and said, "I think I love you."

Ward absorbed that simple statement, which completely changed his carefully planned little speech. He swallowed hard, thought for another two seconds, and responded with, "I think I have loved you since that night in the alley, when you rescued Peters and I by opening the back door holding a dim lantern."

She took one more step forward, which brought them to almost touching, placed her hands on his arms, and raised on her tiptoes. He pulled her closer and they kissed. A kiss that lasted much longer than two seconds.

Two months later…

The following article, written by Henry and Delia (mostly Delia,) appeared in the first July issue of the *Falls Bluff Weekly*:

## PERSONAL

The most exciting event of the summer was the marriage of Henry Stuart Ward and Ardelia Vaughan Simmons on June 25th, 1865, which fell on a Sunday. This came only after careful planning by the bride and her mother as far as proper etiquette was concerned. The main question was: was it required by etiquette that she be married at her parents' home? Her mother concluded that since both parties had been legally married before, and were widowed, it was not a requirement. Therefore, it was decided by the couple that it would be held in the Baptist Church in Falls Bluff. The next concern was about the bride's dress. Letters were exchanged between Delia's mother, Mrs. Vaughan, and Mrs. Ward, Henry's mother, and they ruled that a light blue dress would be proper. Mrs. Vaughan sewed the dress at her home, and brought it with her to Falls Bluff two days before the wedding. Mrs. Ward also came early and they both did the final fitting on Saturday, the day before. Henry's outfit was much less complicated: he simply bought a new suit, which he later called his "business suit." Mr. Vaughan's health was a concern, in that he was somewhat feeble, and walked with difficulty on a cane. On the wedding day, he escorted his daughter down the aisle, with what appeared to be her resting on his arm. The bride's bouquet consisted of blue delphiniums and daisies. Henry was pleased that his brothers and sister came with his mother. His brother, Jonathan, served as his best man. A pleasant surprise was that Mr. Andrew Peters was able to make the trip from Monroe County. Mrs. Vaughan served as matron of honor. The service was conducted by the Rev. T. J. Wilson. It being after Sunday church, most of the town attended the event, filling the church. Mr. Mills, owner of the general store, was generous enough to loan the group a large piece of canvas, which Aaron Phillips and two other lads erected on some corner poles, making a great cover on the church lawn for the food for the reception. The happy couple will honeymoon at the Old White Hotel, in White Sulphur Springs, West Virginia.

## Epilogue

In the months between Ward's return to Falls Bluff and his marriage, the last remnants of the Confederate Army surrendered and dissolved. Gen. Kirby Smith surrendered his Army of the Trans-Mississippi on May 26, 1865. Gen. Stand Watie surrendered his Cherokee and Choctaw Indian Brigade on June 23. On May 29, President Johnson, who succeeded Lincoln, proclaimed a general amnesty. To regain their former legal status, all the men that had been citizens of Old Virginia had to do was swear that they now rejected secession, acknowledged the end of slavery, and were loyal to the United States. Virginia was readmitted to the Union in January of 1870.

**The town of Falls Bluff** recovered from the war. It even grew, although slowly. A church group from Kentucky purchased half of Mr. Mills farm, on the edge of town. They erected a small set of houses, all just alike, and their own church. A magistrate's office was set up in the vacant building between the general store and the newspaper office. A father and son opened a wagon building business off the alley behind the newspaper building. But most important, was the fact that a telegraph office was opened in the little train station in the county seat. Delia was pleased that now she could communicate, (after only a few hours ride,) with some larger newspapers, and receive national news much earlier than before.

In the year following their marriage, on May 15, 1866, **Henry & Delia** were blessed with the birth of a son. There was never any discussion or debating about names. He was named Elijah Stephens Ward. They would call him Eli.

**Drew Peters** rode to Giles County, and after inquiring at the courthouse, found directions to the home of Lige Stephens' parents and delivered the news of his death and gave them Lige's share of the money. He also left Lige's saddlebags and their contents, and handed the unfinished letter to his mother. He immediately wrote a letter to Ward in care of the *Falls Bluff Weekly* informing him. Upon receipt, Ward sat down at his desk and wrote the letter to Lige's parents:

151

Dear Mr. & Mrs. Stephens,

It is with grief that I write to you about the death of your son, Elijah. I understand that Andrew Peters, another soldier who served with Elijah and myself has visited you to personally give you the news of your son's death. As your son's commanding officer for the last two years, it gives me pride to tell you that it was a privilege to have his example of bravery before us. Your son died a true hero, saving the lives of the couple he was staying with, while his broken leg healed. He gave his life saving the lives of that couple, Mr. and Mrs. Zachariah Anderson. He was given a Christian burial by them, and he is buried in their family cemetery, ten miles south of Falls Bluff, Virginia, on the main road, and north of Ridgeton, N.C.

It seems shallow to say that I truly believe that Elijah has gone to a better place, but I do pray that God will assuage your anguish, and leave you only the cherished memory of your son.

Your obedient servant,
Respectfully,
Henry S. Ward
(Late major, 35th Virginia Infantry, CSA)

Drew Peters took over the running of his father's farm, as he had planned. But secretly he longed to be riding again with Major Ward and the squad.

**Michael Thompson** took over the operation of his family's sawmill and grist mill. He reengineered the driving gears based on what he had learned while working on the Owings Mill. He redesigned the cage gear which greatly improved the mill's reliability. Michael decided in his later years to write an account of his clandestine activities during the war. It was widely read throughout the South.

**William Wells** married Sarah Baylous, the girl who had loyally waited for him. They named their first son Henry Stuart Wells. William entered into business with Sarah's brother in a successful sawmill operation. The operation made considerable money in the 1870's and 1880's, buying standing yellow poplar timber, cutting it, and transporting it to their mill. They sold most of their product to the North Carolina furniture companies.

**Harrison Lane** was held by the Union Army in Raleigh, and was pardoned two years after the end of the war. Lane was eventually re-elected governor of North Carolina. After his reelection, he sent his old friend and partner, Mason O'Brien, with part of the bearer bonds to New York to redeem them. The resulting monies went toward helping to rebuild the state's infrastructure.

**Aaron Phillips, a.k.a. "Stonewall,"** the boy spy, became a dedicated employee of the *Falls Bluff Weekly.* He learned typesetting and layout, and took over most of the printing of the newspaper, after Delia and Ward's baby arrived. He became a partner in the newspaper and was a close friend of Delia and Ward for many years.

153

A Page From Major Ward's Code Book:

"B" = behind

"C" = church

"L" = left

"R" = right

"RR" = railroad

"SQ" = squad

(capitol letters) = a building, ie NEWSPAPER = the newspaper building

3 digit number = 1$^{st}$ digit: point on compass (1=north, 2=east, 3= south, 4=west),2$^{nd}$ and 3$^{rd}$ digits = number of yards in that direction.

Signals:
Stroke of the hat brim: "Look out, stay alert, something's up."

Arm down to the side, pointing to the ground: "Ease off, hands off guns."

Clinched right fist in the air, signals: "Stop and hold."

Page 1

Other Books by This Author
(All are historical, non-fiction)

*8th Virginia Cavalry*, (Virginia Regimental Histories Series)
*16th Virginia Cavalry*, (Virginia Regimental Histories Series)
*Better take two guns : the N&W's special agents (railroad detectives)
and their W. Va. Cases*\*^
*Civil War paper items from the Rosanna A. Blake Confederate
Collection*, Marshall University
*Cooney Ricketts : child of the regiment*\*
*Diary of a Confederate Sharpshooter : the life of James Conrad Peters*
*Ely Ensign and the Ensign Manufacturing Company of Huntington,
W.Va.: forerunner of the American Car & Foundry (ACF)*
(Published by Marshall University)
*Gentleman soldier of Greenbottom : the life of Brig. Gen. Albert Gallatin
Jenkins, CSA*\*^
*If I should fall in battle...: the Civil War diary of James P. Stephens
(Company C, 7th Alabama Infantry, CSA)* (Published by
Marshall University)
*Jenkins of Greenbottom : a Civil War saga*
*Last train to Dunlow : history from the hollows of Wayne County, West
Virginia and the coming of the N & W Railroad, 1870-1940*^
*Lumbermen, Log Rafts, and Sawmills: The Lumber and Timber Industry
in Southern West Virginia.* ^
*Murder along the tracks: violent deaths along the Norfolk & Western in
Wayne and Mingo Counties, West Virginia*\*^
*Tattered uniforms and bright bayonets : West Virginia's confederate
soldiers* (Rev. 2^nd^ ed)
*Trail of the Powhatan Arrow : The N & W's Big Sandy Line, Kenova to
Williamson, W. Va.*\*^
*Wayne County, West Virginia in the Civil War*
*Wheels aflame, whistle wide open : train wrecks of the N & W Railroad,
1892-1959*\*^


\*Books available from Amazon.com (as of 9/10/2018)
^ Co-authored by Kay Stamper Dickinson

*In the Beginning...A Legacy of Computing at Marshall University.*

*The Muster Roll of the First Regiment West Virginia Volunteer Infantry, Company K, 1898-1899.*

*Shirking no danger: the Civil War diary of Robert C. Thompson (Lt., Company H, 41st Tennessee Infantry, CSA).*

*Record Book of the Erodelphian and Diagnothian Literary Societies at Marshall Academy and Marshall College 1855-1861.*

*Historic Huntington Businesses: The Birth of Huntington, W.Va., 1871-1900.*

*Harper's Weekly Reports Events of 1865.*

*A Guide to Marshall University Landmarks.*

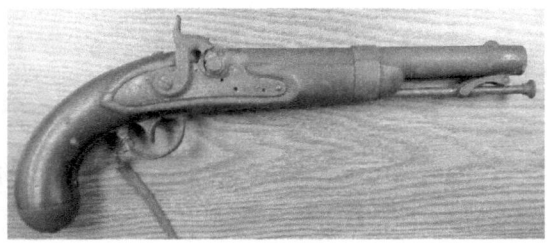

Taggert's horse pistol.